Captain's Dinner Cruise Murder

Dawn Brookes

Captain's Dinner Cruise Murder

A Rachel Prince Mystery

Dawn Brookes

Oakwood Publishing

Paperback Edition 2021
Kindle Edition 2021
Paperback ISBN: 978-1-913065-51-5
Hardback ISBN: 978-1-913065-52-2
Copyright © DAWN BROOKES 2021
Cover Images: AdobeStockImages
Cover Design: Dawn Brookes

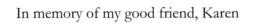

In memory of my good friend, Karen

Chapter 1

Rachel Jacobi-Prince pulled one of the balcony doors open and stepped onto the large, windswept balcony of her suite on deck fifteen. She was once again on board her favourite cruise liner: the luxurious *Coral Queen*. Holding onto the rail, she surveyed the water below as the ship sailed slowly through the Solent. Rachel returned waves to the enthusiastic people aboard smaller vessels, following them to get a closer look as the magnificent liner set sail. The ship's horn warned them away, and they kept to a safe distance.

A draught of cold air blew through her hair from behind. Turning, she was pleased to see the familiar face of Mario, the suite butler. He held the door open, allowing her close friend, Lady Marjorie Snellthorpe, through ahead of him.

Marjorie's spritely steps across the lounge made Rachel smile as she joined her outdoors, swiftly followed by Mario.

"It's a pleasure to see you again, ma'am Rachel. Can I get you ladies anything?" The butler also grinned behind the back of Rachel's octogenarian friend, recognising she was on a mission.

"A pot of tea please, Mario," Marjorie answered first.

"It's good to see you too, Mario," replied Rachel. "I'll have coffee if you have time. I realise you're busy on boarding days."

"I will always have time for you two ladies, don't you worry. I'll be right back." Mario turned and left them on the balcony.

"Have you unpacked?" Marjorie's voice crackled with excited anticipation. Rachel knew how much her friend appreciated her accompanying her on sea voyages from time to time. On this one, though, Marjorie was even more ecstatic because her son had suggested the break and agreed to join them, despite his dislike of cruises.

"Just finished. I thought you'd be with Jeremy and—"

"Tosh, you thought wrong! If that woman has anything to do with it, we won't see them for dust, except when the bills come in."

Jeremy and his 'younger model' wife, as Marjorie insisted on calling her, had expensive tastes. Even Jeremy's spending paled in comparison to that of Octavia Snellthorpe and, according to Marjorie, he struggled to keep pace with it.

"Still, I'm looking forward to meeting her at last," said Rachel, hesitantly.

"Hm, you might not be quite so enthusiastic once you have. Anyway, you won't have long to wait. We're meeting them for dinner."

"In the Coral restaurant, you told me earlier."

"There's been a change of plan; that's what I've come to tell you about." Marjorie's eyes sparkled with excitement, her face flushed.

"Something tells me I might not like what you're about to reveal. Please break it gently if you've organised another surprise murder mystery." The last time Rachel had accompanied Marjorie on a cruise, her friend thought it would be a good idea to enrol them in a series of dinners, which included solving an imaginary murder. In actual fact, the murder had turned out to be real.

"Don't be silly. I learned my lesson on that front. No, it's..." Another gust of wind blew hard, causing Marjorie to lose her footing; she grabbed the balcony rail as Rachel caught hold of her.

"I think we'd better go inside before one of us goes overboard," Rachel chuckled, putting her arm around the shorter woman. It was difficult to reconcile her elderly friend's feisty personality with her slight frame, which sometimes appeared frail.

"It is a little blowy out here," Marjorie agreed.

Mario arrived back after they'd gone inside, with Rachel closing the balcony door behind them. He poured their hot drinks, leaving them on the table before making for the door.

"Let me know if you need anything else, ladies."

"Thank you, Mario," said Marjorie.

The closed door had stopped the draught. "That's better," Rachel picked up her mug, "I could kill a coffee now."

"I'll be pleased to leave this awful weather behind us," Marjorie remarked as she held the saucer in her left hand and the cup in her right. Mario always went to the trouble of ensuring Marjorie had a cup and saucer, knowing how much she hated drinking from mugs. "Hopefully, the Mediterranean will be warmer. It seems to have been a long winter this year."

"It does." Rachel hadn't wanted to take another cruise so soon after the last one, but Marjorie could be very persuasive, particularly when it came to her husband, Carlos, who the elderly lady could play better than a violin. The only consolation was Rachel got to spend quality time with her close friend, and Carlos had promised to decorate the downstairs of their house while she was away.

"I am grateful, Rachel. I know you miss Carlos, but I couldn't face spending the best part of three weeks on a cruise holiday with my daughter-in-law without moral support, especially now." A flicker of a frown overshadowed the previous excitement.

"It's time you told me what's going on." Rachel gulped back a mouthful of coffee. Marjorie would usually disapprove, but she appeared not to notice.

"I'm wondering now if there might be an ulterior motive behind my son and his wife's presence. You know it's not like him to suggest that we take a cruise."

"You think he wants more money?" Rachel quizzed.

Marjorie scoffed. "Jeremy always wants more money, dear. But no, that's not it. He's apparently happened upon some socialite friends of his, people I don't much approve of. Neither did Ralph."

Rachel noticed the glimpse of sadness in her friend's blue eyes. "And you suspect this *chance* meeting might be prearranged?"

Marjorie put down her cup and saucer and rubbed her chin. "I hadn't thought so when he called, but now I'm not so sure. It's hard to say, as the couple in question are regular cruisers and Queen Cruises would be their preferred line. You almost had the misfortune to encounter them on the Mediterranean cruise when you and I first met."

"The one where you were being chased by a hitman?"

"Quite. On that occasion, they had wangled an invitation to the captain's table after somehow hearing I was invited, but then couldn't attend because she was seasick."

"I vaguely remember something like that. You didn't seem happy when they passed themselves off as friends of yours."

"What a remarkable memory you have. Yes, that was it."

"I don't remember their names, though," Rachel confessed.

"I'd be surprised if you did. They are Lord and Lady Fanston. I don't know their first names myself, but they are Jeremy's friends. From what Ralph told me about them, they are greedy show-offs, leeches who have the unfortunate habit of extracting money from gullible people."

"So why does Jeremy like them?"

"Old habits die hard, I'm afraid. He's always been an easy target for people with influence – that's how he managed to get himself tied up with Octavia. She moved in all the right circles; I don't know how because she didn't have a bean before she met Jeremy. She well and truly hooked him, and he took the bait. He may have changed over the past few years, but I'm afraid the impressionable side of him remains his biggest weakness."

"If they cruise regularly and we almost met them on a Mediterranean cruise before, perhaps they are here for the same reason we are, to get a little early spring sunshine. Jeremy might well have met them by chance. He seemed so keen to spend some time with you."

"Exactly. Why the sudden desire to take a cruise when he dislikes them so much?"

"You were excited when you came in, Marjorie. Why this change of mood?"

"I was quite keen, but now I wonder if I'm being a gullible old fool and have been taken for a ride."

Rachel hated seeing her friend's mood swing. It just wasn't like her. "You're not gullible and you're nobody's fool, Marjorie Snellthorpe. Now, are you going to tell me what this change of dinner plan is or will I have to force feed you brandies to extract it from you?"

Marjorie laughed. "Perhaps later, without the force-feeding, if you don't mind. The reason for my excitement is… it's good news in a way. On this occasion, the four of us have an invitation to the captain's table. The bad news is it's courtesy of the Fanstons. We'll be dining with Captain Jenson and the Fanstons at eight. And, I expect, that wretched chief of security is likely to be there."

Rachel smiled. Marjorie's historic love-hate relationship with Jack Waverley, the security chief, often created tension, and the poor man blustered and stumbled over his words whenever she was around.

"You need to go easy on him if he is there." Rachel exhaled slowly, remembering who wouldn't be there. "Shame Sarah isn't on board." Her best friend, cruise ship nurse, Sarah Bradshaw, was in England preparing for her wedding.

"I know. It won't be the same without seeing her and Jason. I'm very much looking forward to the wedding when we get back. Will you be helping with preparations?"

"Not until the weekend before. Sarah's mum isn't letting anyone else get much of a look in." Rachel didn't mention how much work both she, as a detective sergeant in the police, and Carlos as a private investigator, had on;

she didn't want Marjorie to feel guilty about inviting her on the cruise.

"Much to Sarah's annoyance, no doubt."

"It depends whether you consider threatening to call the wedding off, elope to Australia or put sedatives in her mother's tea annoyed."

Marjorie cackled loudly, and Rachel joined in.

"Weddings are supposed to be such joyous occasions, but sometimes they're just too stressful," Marjorie remarked.

"I'm exaggerating, of course. Sarah's so much in love and looking forward to marrying Jason, even Mary Bradshaw's efforts won't dampen her spirits for too long. Besides, Mary means well. She just needs to back off a bit, that's all. I suppose it's a mother's prerogative to try to make everything perfect for their offspring's wedding."

"I don't believe your mother got quite so involved with your wedding, did she?"

"To some extent she did, but Dad's job keeps her busy enough. And unlike me, Sarah's an only child."

"True. I assume your father will be officiating over the happy couple? I forgot to ask."

"Yep. Sarah grew up in the same village as me, and with Sarah's parents still living there, Dad's church seemed the natural choice. Jason doesn't seem to mind."

The cloud that had been gathering over Marjorie regarding her son's motives for being on the cruise had disappeared momentarily.

"I was delighted to receive an invitation to the wedding. I'm so looking forward to it, and to meeting your parents again. It was interesting spending time with Susan and Brendan on the Caribbean cruise."

"It would have been better without the murder and having to conceal my involvement from my mother."

"Murders plural, if my memory serves me right." They laughed again.

Rachel remembered how fond her parents had grown of Marjorie during that holiday. She had hoped this one would bring Marjorie and Jeremy closer. Their relationship could be described as strong, but not close. Jeremy was aloof at times and had a tendency to be blunt, but Rachel was certain he loved his mother underneath it all. She hoped he didn't ruin the opportunity chasing some fantasy concocted by Lord and Lady Fanston; she wasn't much looking forward to meeting them after Marjorie's description.

Hopefully, it's just a coincidence they're on the same cruise.

Chapter 2

Rachel and Marjorie arrived at the private function room on deck seven. Marjorie, as always, was immaculately turned out in a mid-tone cream below-knee wrap skirt with a jacket to match. Her white evening bag and sandals finished the outfit, making her look every bit the lady she was. They were greeted at the entrance by a skinny, clean-shaven uniformed officer neither had met before.

"Good evening, ladies. Could I see your tickets, please?"

Marjorie raised a quizzical eyebrow. "I'm sorry, we don't have tickets. We were invited to dinner by Lord and Lady Fanston through my son, Jeremy Snellthorpe."

"Could I take your names, please?"

"Marjorie Snellthorpe and Rachel Jacobi-Prince."

The officer's green eyes scanned his list. "I'm sorry, Mrs Snellthorpe, but I don't see your names. Guests aren't allowed to invite other people to the captain's dinner.

There must be some mistake." His pleasant Irish brogue didn't hide the fact he was not to be trifled with.

"It's Lady Snellthorpe, not Mrs. Will you please look again?" demanded Marjorie.

The confused-looking officer shook his head after scanning the list once more. Rachel felt sorry for him as Marjorie let out an exasperated sigh.

"Perhaps you could check with Lord and Lady Fanston, erm… Officer Flame?" Rachel suggested, consulting his name badge. The officer scanned the room behind him, after looking once more at his list.

Marjorie nudged Rachel in the ribs, whispering, "I hope he's not in charge of fire safety."

"Stop it, Marjorie, don't set me off," Rachel spluttered. She watched the flustered man, still not moving out of their way, clearly debating with himself what to do next.

"I apologise, but Lord and Lady Fanston haven't arrived yet, and even if they had, I still wouldn't be able to allow you into the party without the captain's permission."

Officer Flame was saved any further embarrassment by the familiar voice of the chief medical officer.

"Lady Marjorie, Rachel," Dr Graham Bentley broke through the standoff. "How good to see you. Are you dining with us this evening?"

"If we can get past this young man," Marjorie chortled. "He seems to think we are interlopers."

Officer Flame's face turned crimson, matching his name. "I, erm…"

Dr Bentley squeezed the man's shoulder. "Don't worry, Flame. I can vouch for these two."

"But they're not on the list, sir."

"Really? How catastrophic. Give me the list."

Flame handed the clipboard to his senior officer, who took a fountain pen from his upper pocket and wrote the two names down.

"There you are, Flame, no harm done. This way, ladies."

Officer Flame reluctantly stepped aside, allowing Marjorie and Rachel access into the forbidden territory.

"Sorry about that. Flame's a rather serious sort," said Dr Bentley.

"We should have told him Jeremy and Octavia will be arriving soon," said Rachel.

"Jeremy can fight his own battles. Thank heavens you arrived, Dr Bentley; I thought Rachel was going to have to karate chop the man."

"I don't think it would have come to that." Dr Bentley grinned as Rachel nudged her friend to behave.

"He was just doing his job, Marjorie. We can't blame him for that."

"I suppose not, but he reminded me of a younger version of Chief Waverley."

"Unforgivable," Rachel laughed.

Dr Bentley stopped to take champagne from a waiter, offering the two women full glasses before taking one for himself. When aperitifs were in their hands, the doctor's eyes brightened. Smiling, he held up his glass.

"Welcome aboard. They warned me you two were on the passenger list. Now, can you explain why you're gatecrashing the captain's dinner?"

"I've never gatecrashed anything in my life, dear doctor. We are here by invitation. At least, that's what I was led to believe. I do hope Jeremy is not playing jokes on his poor mother or we could be in for a rather embarrassing evening."

Dr Bentley's forehead creased. Rachel explained.

"Marjorie's son, Jeremy, and his wife are also on board. They ran into some old friends, Lord and Lady Fanston, who invited them, and by default, us, to join them here for dinner. I do hope they asked the captain first."

"So do I," said Dr Bentley. "He's heading this way now."

"Lady Marjorie, Mrs Jacobi-Prince. Lord and Lady Fanston told me to expect extra guests. It's a pleasure to have you both on board the *Coral Queen* again." The enigmatic Captain Jenson lowered his voice. "As long as you haven't brought any murderers with you."

"Now, now, Captain, don't go spoiling the fun." Marjorie chortled while Rachel felt her face flush at the reference to the frequency of the investigations she'd become involved with aboard her beloved cruise ship.

"Are you friends of Lord and Lady Fanston?" Captain Jenson asked.

"Not really; I've only met them once, but I believe my son and his wife know them. They bumped into each other after boarding, and here we are. I don't believe they have arrived yet?"

"Neither the Fanstons nor your son have arrived up to now, but I've just met your engaging daughter-in-law. She's over there with some of Lord and Lady Fanston's guests." Captain Jenson nodded toward two groups of people. Octavia, who Rachel recognised from photographs, stood out in a short, tightly fitting bright-red cocktail dress. She was an attractive woman in her early forties, with long auburn hair and full lips. Six-inch stiletto heels caused her to tower over one of the two men she was talking to. Rachel's observant eyes also noticed an older woman in a jade green evening dress having an intense conversation with another woman who appeared to be in her forties.

Diamond wedding balloons drew her attention away from the gathering.

"Is it an anniversary celebration?"

"Yes, it's Lord and Lady Fanston's diamond wedding, although why they would want to spend it at my humble table beats me. I usually leave these dinners to my deputy if I'm honest, but my presence was a condition of the booking, and it appears Lord Fanston knows who to influence to get his own way."

Marjorie clinked her glass with the captain's. "That sense of entitlement comes with hereditary peerage sometimes. I think that's the Fanstons in a nutshell." She winked. "Let's drink to us all being reluctant guests."

Captain Jenson grimaced. "I'm sorry if I spoke out of turn, I didn't mean any offence. And you forget, Lady Snellthorpe, I'm to be the enthusiastic host."

Rachel had always assumed the cruise ship captain was an extrovert from previous meetings when he had mingled warmly with guests and had his photograph taken ad infinitum.

"You might dupe Rachel, Captain, but I've been around the block a few times. You love every minute of it."

"Sometimes I do, Lady Marjorie. Please don't tell anyone, but I'm not a huge fan of hosting dinners. I don't always know what to say; I fear being a disappointment. Does that sound pathetic?"

"A little, but we won't hold it against you. Trust me, you won't be a disappointment tonight. The Fanstons will dine out on the occasion for months."

"Marjorie!" Rachel chastised her friend. "We don't know them, so let's keep an open mind, shall we?"

"Quite right," Captain Jenson smiled warmly. "Not everyone's as cynical as you are, Lady Marjorie."

"Enough of the Lady business, please. Actually, I'm rather looking forward to the evening. I'd love to introduce you to my son."

"And I look forward to you doing so."

"Who are those men Octavia's talking to?"

Rachel's attention was drawn again to Octavia. The two men she was having an animated conversation with appeared to be in their fifties. The women Rachel had noticed earlier were engaged in what now seemed to be a heated discussion on the fringes.

"They are all relatives of Lord and Lady Fanston. The short, casually dressed fellow is their son, who goes by a different surname, I believe. Mr Thomas Elrod."

Marjorie's interest was clearly piqued. "That's interesting, not Lord Thomas Fanston. Peers' sons usually take the honorary title. Was he adopted or was Lady Fanston married before?"

"That I couldn't tell you," answered the captain. "Unlike yourself, Lady... erm... Marjorie, and Rachel here, I'm no detective."

"Rather underdressed, isn't he? He must think the shabby-chic look is still in."

Rachel had also observed the out-of-place Bermuda shorts and brightly coloured shirt, as well as shoulder-length wavy grey hair and longish beard and moustache.

"He reminds me of a younger Richard Branson," she remarked.

"You're right, Rachel, but the entrepreneurial billionaire doesn't need to dress to impress. I suspect Mr Elrod isn't anywhere near as wealthy."

"Don't be a snob, Marjorie. Perhaps he's a mature rebel. I think he's rather attractive for his age."

"If you like that sort of thing. And what do you mean, for his age? He can't be more than sixty – that's young in my book," countered Marjorie.

"I'd say late fifties," said Rachel.

"Now you're showing off."

"What about the other man?" The taller man, who appeared younger than Thomas, had cropped brown hair and wore an ill-fitting suit. He looked to be flirting with Octavia Snellthorpe.

"That's Lord Wilfred Vanmeter: Lady Fanston's nephew, I believe. His mother, Lady Vanmeter, is chatting with Mr Elrod's wife."

Rachel again looked at the two women, who appeared to be arguing in hushed tones while the men and Octavia remained oblivious.

"More lords and ladies than I can keep up with," chuckled Marjorie.

"You must explain one day how you get these titles, Marjorie. I can't keep up."

"It's a complicated business, Rachel. There are five ranks of the peerage, and sons and daughters, plus in-laws, inherit courtesy titles. Hence, there are thousands of lords and ladies up and down the land. I believe Lord Fanston is a baron, as was Ralph. My title comes from my father, who was a duke, but I would have become Lady anyway on marrying Ralph. It really is…"

The sound of her daughter-in-law's raucous laugh interrupted Marjorie's attention. She straightened her back.

"Would you excuse us please, Captain Jenson? I think it's time I introduced Rachel to Octavia."

Captain Jenson removed his cap, revealing a thick crop of black hair. "Of course." He looked at his watch. "The guests of honour should be here soon."

Rachel was certain Octavia Snellthorpe had looked their way a couple of times during their conversation with the captain, but had made no effort to greet Marjorie, or even cast a smile in her mother-in-law's direction. It didn't put her at the top of Rachel's would-be friends list. The woman was also blatantly encouraging the Vanmeter man to flirt, as far as Rachel could tell, and he was lapping up the opportunity as he brushed his hand against Octavia's arm for a few moments longer than was appropriate. Marjorie's sharp eyes, no doubt, hadn't missed the signals either.

Lord Wilfred Vanmeter turned impatiently towards them as they arrived on the scene and Marjorie coughed. He looked down at her, then his bloodshot eyes lit up when he turned his gaze to Rachel. She sighed inwardly.

Don't even think about it, I've met so many of your type before.

Octavia's flirtatious grin transformed into a false smile as she acknowledged Marjorie. Making a display of bending down to the small-statured woman, she delivered a pretentious air-kiss.

"Good evening, Mother."

"Octavia," Marjorie returned stiffly.

"How good to see you. Sorry we couldn't join you on the journey down to the port; Jeremy insisted on bringing the Jaguar. You know how men are." Octavia giggled as she turned her gaze back towards Wilfred Vanmeter, who laughed like a hyena.

Seriously! thought Rachel. *Have I just returned to school?*

"This is Rachel, my dear friend." Marjorie's voice cut through the melodrama. "Rachel, this is Octavia, my daughter-*in-law*." The emphasis wasn't lost on Rachel.

"Nice to meet you at last. Marjorie's told me so much about you." Rachel held out her hand. Octavia frowned, taking the proffered hand with her fingertips, and releasing it again as if it were a hot coal.

"Likewise," she said.

The awkwardness was interrupted by the Fanstons' son. "Hello, I'm Tom," he said. "You must be Lady Snellthorpe. My mother told me you'd be joining us for dinner. What a pleasure to meet you at last. I've met Jeremy a few times and I had the good fortune to meet your husband a few years back. Such a charming man."

Marjorie's eyes moistened just long enough for Rachel to notice as Thomas Elrod turned his attention towards her.

"Good to meet you too, Rachel. Jeremy tells me what a help you've been to his mother."

Unlike Octavia's, Thomas's smile was genuine, reaching his wide brown eyes. His rugged looks juxtaposed with his charming manner; his handshake was warm and confident. She liked him.

"This is my cousin, Wilf, my wife, Annette, and my aunt Melody."

The two women had apparently called a truce on their discussion as soon as Marjorie and Rachel joined the party.

"Charmed, I'm sure," Wilfred addressed Rachel first, holding onto her hand and giving it a squeeze that sent an unpleasant shiver down her spine. She pulled away, avoiding any eye contact with the man.

"Oh Wilfred, do stop with your flirting. Can't you see these women are wearing wedding rings?" Lady Vanmeter glared at Octavia and smiled apologetically towards Rachel before greeting Marjorie. "Pleased to meet you, Lady Marjorie. My sister has mentioned you on several occasions."

Marjorie appeared taken aback. Rachel knew that Lady Fanston was a friend of Jeremy's rather than Marjorie's. Was some sort of plot being hatched here, of which her friend was blissfully unaware?

"I've only met your sister once before at a fundraising event organised by my late husband," replied Marjorie. "I must admit, it surprised me to be invited to join you all at the captain's table, especially as I now understand it's a special celebration. You might be mistaking me with my son and daughter-in-law. They know your sister and her husband well."

"Oh, really? I was led to believe you and your husband were her close friends. My sister is prone to exaggeration."

"As I said, my son knows her well, so perhaps that's where the confusion lies."

Melody Vanmeter snorted sceptically. "Perhaps."

Annette Elrod hadn't said a word, Rachel noticed. She suspected this was going to be a long evening.

Chapter 3

Rachel was already tiring of Wilfred Vanmeter's attempts at getting her attention. He reeked of alcohol and cigar smoke and tended to lean in closer than was comfortable. His mother was commandeering Marjorie and the apparently reluctant Octavia. The latter woman glared at Rachel every so often, clearly unhappy that Rachel had become the centre of Wilfred and Tom's attention. Octavia also scowled in Marjorie's direction at every opportunity. Marjorie was mostly ignoring her.

Octavia had nothing to be jealous of as far as Rachel was concerned: she was enjoying Tom's company much more than his cousin's. Tom was just telling her a funny story when Wilfred butted in again, trying to shove Tom out of the way so he could move in on her.

"Back off, Wilf. Take the hint: she's not interested. Go and get yourself a coffee or something." Tom's annoyance told Rachel she wasn't the only one tiring of the lanky man with bulging bloodshot eyes.

"You can't talk. You're far too old for her. He's nearly sixty, you know," Wilfred slurred, wagging his finger at Tom before heading in Annette Elrod's direction.

"Sorry about him. He doesn't know when to stop flirting; or drinking, for that matter, especially when the liquor's free."

"I've met worse," said Rachel.

"I bet you have with looks like yours. Sorry, I don't mean to offend, but your husband's a lucky man." Tom sounded miserable as he looked over to where his wife appeared to be having a joint moaning session with Melody and Wilfred. Freed from Melody's attentions, Marjorie was now chatting with Octavia, who didn't appear to be listening, keeping her eyes focussed on Wilfred.

"I'm lucky too. I couldn't ask for a better husband. How about you?"

Tom shrugged. "Happy enough, I suppose, considering we're trapped."

"What do you mean?" asked Rachel, but there was no time to hear a reply as Lord and Lady Fanston's arrival was announced. Jeremy accompanied them.

Tom's jaw visibly dropped, his wide brown eyes squinting at his mother. It was easy for Rachel to see why. The elegantly dressed Lady Fanston, who appeared to be in her late seventies, had successfully captured everyone's attention. She swirled her slim arms around as if she was royalty, looking gorgeous in a long, flowing sea-blue evening dress. Yet, it wasn't her dress that was eye-catching, but a dazzling diamond necklace reflecting light from the chandeliers, as were two huge diamond earrings.

Marjorie shuffled to Rachel's side. "If they're real, she's wearing a million pounds' worth of jewellery around her neck alone. I was under the impression they were both relatively penniless."

The spell that the bejewelled entrance had cast was broken when Captain Jenson walked over to greet the guests of honour. Melody Vanmeter's disapproving voice could be heard above the murmuring crowd.

"Now that we're all here, I think we should eat. We've already kept the captain waiting far too long, and the champagne's going to some of our heads." She looked disparagingly over at her son, whose green eyes had seemingly forgotten about anything other than the diamond necklace.

"Even you can't compete with those diamonds," Marjorie whispered.

"Thank God," said Rachel. "Octavia seems pretty besotted with them too."

Marjorie tutted. "Silly woman. Some people are never satisfied with what they have, are they?" She looked sorrowfully towards her son.

The only person who appeared more annoyed than bedazzled by the jewellery was Tom. Rachel overheard him muttering on the way through to dinner, "What are you up to, Mother?"

Lady Fanston patted him on the arm. "I don't know what you mean, darling."

Jeremy joined Rachel and Marjorie for the short walk to the room next door, where a large round table was beautifully laid out, ready and waiting for the guests.

"Hello, Mother," he kissed Marjorie on the cheek. "Hello, Rachel, good to see you again. Sorry we're late. Harvey and I were talking a bit of business while waiting for Colleen to get ready. We lost track of time."

Jeremy looked the part in his black tuxedo jacket with satin lapels, matching trousers, and silk bow tie, but the surroundings clearly overawed him. He had also been drinking, judging by the alcohol fumes.

"Harvey and Colleen?" Marjorie replied. "I didn't know their first names. Those diamonds look real – are they?"

"What diamonds? Oh, those. I can't say I noticed." Jeremy fiddled with his collar, his face flushing enough to tell Rachel he was lying.

"Jeremy, don't play me for a fool. Of course you noticed."

"Okay, I noticed, and although I didn't ask, yes, I believe they are real."

The three of them had fallen back from the primary group, so Marjorie stopped to challenge her son. "I was under the impression the Fanstons weren't wealthy?"

"They have both money and connections, Mother. Please don't be difficult. Harvey's got a proposition to make that will benefit us both."

Jeremy couldn't have done more damage if he'd hit his mother. The colour drained from Marjorie's face as the realisation that she had fallen for a ruse to do business, along with the disappointment, set in.

"Hence the cruise, I suppose?" Before Jeremy had the chance to reply, Marjorie took Rachel's arm. "We'd better join the captain's table before anything else untoward happens." Turning to her son, she said, "It's time to grow up, Jeremy. You're being taken for a ride."

Jeremy's face reddened, his cheeks puffing out as he bulldozed past them to join his wife in the empty space between her and Harvey Fanston.

"It appears my ideal holiday has taken a turn for the worse, my dear," Marjorie said quietly as they made their way through to dinner. Rachel said nothing. Although she was fuming at Jeremy about the hurt, he was inadvertently causing his mother. She would never get between the two of them. Perhaps the untimely proposition would turn out to be a good one, but somehow, she doubted that very much.

Chapter 4

Marjorie was seated next to Lady Fanston, and Rachel took the seat on Marjorie's right, delighted to be next to Captain Jenson on the other side. Lord Harvey Fanston was next to his wife, with Jeremy next to him. Rachel was relieved to see Wilfred Vanmeter far away, on the opposite side of the table, sandwiched between Annette Elrod and his mother. Thomas, or Tom as he'd introduced himself, was next to his wife on one side and Dr Bentley on his left. They had placed Octavia next to Melody Vanmeter, completing the circle of twelve.

As far as Rachel could determine, the mystery necklace and earrings remained the centre of unspoken attention throughout dinner. Every so often, one of the guests' eyes would be drawn to the sparkling exhibits adorning the weather-beaten, dry, wrinkled neck and lengthy earlobes of the wearer.

Captain Jenson flashed Rachel a grin. Lowering his voice, he whispered, "If I get lost for words, I'm relying on you to bail me out."

Rachel had barely spoken two sentences to the captain on previous cruises despite several meetings, but now he made her feel like they were old friends sharing a secret. No doubt this was in part a result of her solving crimes aboard his ship.

"I'll do my best, Captain, but I don't like to be centre of attention either. I'm not a fan of crowds, probably because I spent too much time as a beat officer breaking them up or holding lines separating rival protests."

"In that case, we'll help each other out, or I'll defer to the good doctor on my right. Oh, and please feel free to call me Peter."

"I couldn't possibly. It wouldn't feel right. I still call Dr Bentley Dr Bentley, although Sarah and the medical staff call him Graham."

"Next, you'll be telling me you call your father Vicar."

Rachel chuckled. "No, he's just Dad."

Conversations hushed for a short while as the guests studied the à la carte menu. Dinners were always top notch on board the *Coral Queen* and Rachel suspected the Fanstons would want to get their money's worth this evening. Notwithstanding that, she was beginning to think the rumour of them being mere socialites wasn't true.

An efficient head waiter took the captain's order first, followed by each of the guests, making recommendations when asked, otherwise waiting patiently. His patience must have been tested to the limit when it came to Wilfred and Melody Vanmeter, who seemed to take an age to decide on a main course. Rachel had opted for a seasonal fruit medley to start with and almond crusted haddock with aubergine, bell peppers and a creamy lemon sauce as her main. She had heard Marjorie order French onion soup with croutons as a starter and Steak Diane for her main. When she cast a glance Marjorie's way to check she was okay, it appeared she was enjoying an amicable conversation with Lady Fanston.

That's good to see.

Captain Jenson drew her attention away once more as the waiter finally got an order from the Vanmeters and made his way around the rest of the table.

"I didn't get the opportunity to thank you personally for helping Jack Waverley track down our saboteur during the New Year's outing. Not to mention the other matter." 'The other matter' being the murder of the head of health and fitness the first night on board.

"I was pleased to be able to help. Where is the security chief? I thought he might be here."

"So did I. He must have heard you were coming and made himself scarce." Captain Jenson laughed at his own joke.

"He's been called to deal with a crew matter," Dr Bentley chipped in. "Sorry to butt in, but I overheard you mention Jack."

Captain Jenson frowned. "I hope it's not trouble brewing."

"Just a minor fracas, I believe, nothing to concern us."

"Is everything quiet on the medical front?"

"Yes, we're quiet so far tonight. Our interim nurse, Mitchell Timms, is on call along with Janet for the medics."

"Janet Plover's turned out to be a good pick, hasn't she? I hope you'll be able to hang on to her."

Rachel had met Janet, the junior doctor, a capable and efficient Welsh bundle of energy who lit up a room with her enthusiasm. They had bonded during the last two cruises, encountering each other in a professional and personal capacity.

The captain and Dr Bentley talked shop for a while, giving Rachel the opportunity to study the mismatched gathering in more detail. She sensed unarticulated tension around the table, perceiving agitation and frayed tempers smouldering beneath the loud and apparently friendly banter. Family gatherings tended to be difficult or pleasant. This one was turning out to be the former.

Jeremy was engrossed in conversation with Lord Fanston while Octavia appeared none too happy with being stuck next to Melody Vanmeter. Their conversation appeared more stilted than others around the table. Wilfred gave Octavia the occasional 'I'm still interested' look, but even that didn't draw a smile from the woman. Marjorie had explained to Rachel that her daughter-in-law liked to be the centre of attention.

Tom occasionally glared in the direction of his mother, clearly trying to have an unspoken conversation with her. From the way he inclined his head towards the necklace, that's what seemed to be the issue. Rachel wondered why it should annoy him so much, unless he was concerned Lady Fanston was being extravagant. She shook her head, bemused.

"Are you all right, dear?" Marjorie enquired.

"I'm fine, thanks." She wanted to say she couldn't wait for dinner to be over, but she was at least enjoying Captain Jenson and Dr Bentley's company. "How about you?"

"So, so." Marjorie lowered her voice. "She tells me the necklace and earrings are real, but all is not as it seems, I fear. I'm trying to find out what's going on, but not getting very far, I'm afraid. We'll compare notes later."

Rachel couldn't imagine wearing something that valuable so openly, which made it highly likely she would never want to own anything like it. Not that she was in any danger of doing so on a police salary. What would be the point of owning something, only to lock it away, never to be seen?

"Interesting she brought the jewellery on the cruise. I'd be terrified it would get damaged or stolen," was all she could think of to say.

Marjorie didn't get the opportunity to reply as Lady Fanston tugged at her arm, clearly not about to let her out of her clutches, having probably ensured she was placed next to her.

"Marjorie, you and I are going to be such good friends. There are so many people I'd like to introduce you to."

Marjorie gave Rachel an eye-roll, whispering, "I'd better speak to the tiresome woman." Sighing, she then turned her attention back in Lady Fanston's direction.

Starters arrived soon afterwards. Perhaps the food would help soak up some of the alcohol that everyone around the table had heartily imbibed except for Rachel, the captain and Dr Bentley. Even Marjorie was drinking more than she usually did.

Dutch courage, no doubt, thought Rachel.

"It's a shame Sarah isn't on board," Captain Jenson said, knowing Rachel and Sarah were best friends. "Have you seen much of her since she's taken her break?"

"Not as much as I'd like to. I live in Leicester now and work's been full-on, but she and Jason did come and stay overnight when they were on their way up north to see his parents."

"I hope for Graham and Jack's sake they come back after they're married."

Jason was a security officer and had turned out to be a trusted confidant to Chief Waverley. Sarah was indispensable in the medical team, according to Dr Bentley.

"They gave me the impression they would be." Rachel would love to have them live close to her and Carlos, but knew they both enjoyed their work aboard the *Coral Queen*.

"There would always be a place for you as part of Jack's team, you know. Carlos too – I hear he's a talented investigator."

"Thank you, Captain. Chief Waverley has offered me a job on several occasions, but it's never been the right time. Carlos's business is expanding so, if you'll excuse the pun, I think that ship may have sailed."

"Shame."

"I'm surprised Lady Fanston isn't sitting next to you," Rachel changed the subject.

"I do have some control over proceedings, despite being wheeled out and put on display to all and sundry."

Rachel laughed again. Captain Jenson appeared to have a dry sense of humour, and she was warming to it.

Conversations became more intense, almost fierce, during dinner. The food wasn't enough to soak up the amount of wine being drunk, in addition to the aperitifs already consumed. She suspected the captain's presence was the only factor keeping a lid on things, thereby preventing the anger from spilling over.

This is going to become unpleasant. I just hope they don't invite us to any after-dinner celebrations.

Chapter 5

Lady Fanston hogged Captain Jenson's attention for most of the after-dinner conversation, leaving him little time to circulate among the other guests before he excused himself, returning to the bridge. As soon as he and Dr Bentley left, the anniversary guests returned to the function room where a live band was now playing. A few other organised parties combined with theirs, crowding the room.

Surprisingly, Marjorie appeared happy to stay, even as the bickering among the Fanston party came and went. Lady Fanston continued holding court as if she were royalty, with Jeremy and Octavia being chief cheerleaders.

Marjorie tutted.

"Why are we still here?" Rachel muttered when she managed to get her friend alone.

"Sorry, dear. I just want to see what Lord and Lady Fanston are up to and what influence they are wielding over my son. I also want to keep an eye on *her*." Marjorie inclined her head towards Octavia, who was once more playing off the two men, Tom and Wilf, despite Tom's wife's presence.

"I'm surprised Annette Elrod doesn't put a stop to it. Although Wilf appears to be the one who's interested."

"From what I've observed, I don't believe Annette Elrod much cares. Rachel, I'm not sure what's happening here, but they all seem bedazzled by the Fanstons and those wretched diamonds. Watch how their eyes keep them in sight; even Octavia, with all her flirting, is only at it half-heartedly. I fear her icy heart is concocting something."

"Really? Do you think it's like the fever of the California Gold Rush?" Rachel tried to lighten the mood. The undercurrent stirred up by the presence of the diamonds hadn't escaped her notice.

"What do you know about that?"

"You forget, I studied history. Dad and I always talk about historical events whenever we get together; we bore Mum to death. There were two gold rushes around the same time. California's began in 1848 and the Australian one in 1851."

"I wish I had your penchant for remembering facts and dates," said Marjorie. "I have heard of gold fever, but now we appear to have diamond fever."

"Also a recognised term, mainly associated with South Africa."

"Now you're just being a show-off," Marjorie chuckled.

"Okay, so what would you like to do about this? Because I don't want to be around these people for much longer. Tom's all right, but the rest... Oh, I'm sorry, Marjorie..." Rachel's hand went to her mouth.

"Don't worry, I understand. My son's under the influence, I'm afraid. It's not wealth – he has that, or will have when I'm gone; it's the prestige and power he's overawed with. But as far as I'm aware, Lord and Lady Fanston are parasites. I don't know where those diamonds have come from, but unless I'm badly misinformed, they are not hers."

Rachel rubbed her temples, feeling a headache coming on. "What makes you say that?"

"My dear friends Kenneth and Philomena Rainworth tell me the Fanstons have no money to speak of, so, despite the glitz and glamour of this evening, I know who I believe."

Rachel wondered if Marjorie's friends could be mistaken, but trusted her judgement when it came to people. "Well, we're not going to find out much standing here. Shall we split up and see if we can wheedle some information from the others about what Lord Fanston's proposing? That's assuming you don't want to just ask your son and Lord Fanston outright... Maybe we'll resolve the diamond paradox at the same time, but I can't say I'm much interested in them other than why she would choose to wear them so publicly if they are worth as much as you think they are."

"I'm certainly not going to ask the Fanstons or Jeremy about their plans! I wouldn't give them the satisfaction. Besides, I never discuss business when I'm on holiday."

"That's like me saying I never investigate murder when on holiday."

Marjorie giggled before gripping her arm. "I'll take Wilf and Tom. You'll need to distract Octavia."

Rachel swallowed down the lump in her throat. "It's not me she's interested in."

"Don't be defeatist, Rachel, it's not like you. I can't leave you with the drunk and amorous Wilf, can I? Carlos would never forgive me."

"I suppose you're right. What about Jeremy and the Fanstons?"

"Once you're finished with Octavia, perhaps you could have a go at Lady Fanston. She and her sister seem to be at odds at the moment. I don't think we'll get anything out of Mrs Elrod, she's rather a mouselike creature."

Except when she's with Melody Vanmeter, Rachel thought.

"You owe me after this, Marjorie Snellthorpe."

"Add it to my tab," Marjorie's sparkling blue eyes were energised as she headed towards Tom and Wilf.

Rachel inhaled a deep breath and followed her friend, diverting from the men and heading towards Octavia. Marjorie's years of experience as a titled lady and the wife of a successful businessman came to the fore as she sandwiched herself between her targets. Octavia Snellthorpe was no match for her mother-in-law, but she was going to try. Rachel stealthily stepped between her and the trio.

"I love that dress," she said. "The colour really suits you."

Octavia's heels gave her a slight edge in height, but not in determination. She capitulated.

"Thanks, it's a Coco Chanel. She's the best in my opinion."

Dress designers weren't high on Rachel's knowledge list, so she nodded, moving on to safer ground.

"How do you find the ship?"

"Impressive. I can't understand why Jeremy hasn't brought me on a cruise before. I'll be having words with him later."

"Cruising's not for everyone. Marjorie loves them, of course, and I hear Lord and Lady Fanston are frequent cruisers."

"Are they now? I'm surprised I wasn't told. Something else I need to speak to Jeremy about."

"Do you know the Fanstons well?"

"Very well. Harvey and Jeremy have been doing a lot of business together of late. Colleen and I like the same things. We frequent the same dinner parties within our circle. I don't suppose you've met them before, not mixing in the same league."

Rachel ignored the condescending sneer. Warning bells sounded loudly in her head.

"What business is Lord Fanston in?"

"I believe he's an investor rather than a businessman. He doesn't need to work. If I'm honest, I find Jeremy's obsession with business boring."

Not the proceeds, though, thought Rachel. "Jeremy mentioned Lord Fanston had a proposition for Marjorie before we went in to dinner, sounded like it might be something exciting."

"There is something in the pipeline. That's why Jeremy insisted we come on the cruise. I wasn't keen, except Colleen convinced me it would be fun, and now I'm here… well, I'm not complaining."

That confirms one answer Marjorie won't like, Rachel thought as she persevered.

"Did Jeremy mention what all the excitement was about?"

Octavia's eyes narrowed. "Why are you so interested in my husband's business dealings?"

"I'm not really, I'm just making conversation."

"Must be an occupational hazard, I guess, being nosy. I hear you're a policewoman, so you must have to poke your nose into other people's business all the time."

Ignoring the second barb, Rachel tried a different tack. "I'm surprised your husband doesn't discuss important matters with you. Don't tell me Jeremy's one of those men who thinks a woman's place is playing hostess and shopping. I wouldn't have thought Marjorie would approve, being very much head of the business, even though she allows Jeremy to manage things."

"That's just the trouble, isn't it? *Some* women should get out of the way. Jeremy's quite capable of making business decisions, but his blasted mother has to sign off on every major deal. And for your information, I do know what it's all about; it's—"

Octavia's attention was suddenly taken up with the arrival of Wilf, who had seemingly managed to give Marjorie the slip.

"What are you two beauties talking about?"

Octavia poked him in the chest, pouting her full lips and pretend-stumbling closer to him. "Wouldn't you like to know?" She batted her false eyelashes and gazed into his eyes mischievously.

"I would indeed," he touched her bare arm.

Rachel wanted to throw up or bang their heads together, but she left the couple to flirt, feeling almost sorry for Jeremy. She had grown to like him over the past few years after an inauspicious start, but now she was angry. Thank heavens Marjorie's late husband had the foresight to leave his wife controlling interest in the firm, something Jeremy made his feelings known about whenever he couldn't get his own way. If he thought manipulating his mother was going to work, he didn't know her at all. Whatever the deal, Marjorie would dig her heels in. She wasn't one who would be taken for a ride.

Chapter 6

Marjorie wriggled her way in between Octavia, Wilfred, and Tom. Both men moved aside to allow her space, although Marjorie noticed Wilfred moving with far less grace than Tom.

Giving them her tried and tested 'fascinated and interested' look, she began, "I'd love to hear more about the two of you," Marjorie's keen eye caught that of Rachel as the younger woman steered Octavia to one side. "Lady Fanston mentioned over dinner how you grew up together."

"Wilf's mother was widowed quite early in her marriage and we lived close by, so we played together as boys," Tom explained.

"That was a long time ago. And it's Wilfred, not Wilf, Lady Marjorie. He only calls me that to irritate me."

"Understood. I take it you've gone your separate ways since? Still, early friendships are forged in stone, aren't they? That's what my father used to say."

"Maybe they are sometimes, or maybe not," Wilfred glared at Thomas.

"We don't live close to each other nowadays, Lady Marjorie. Annette and I live in Lincolnshire; London doesn't suit us at all. I'm afraid it has always annoyed Wilf here that I got the girl."

"Your wife?" Marjorie raised a quizzical eyebrow.

"Yes. Not that he appreciates her one jot. It was all about the competition. Tom always has to win. But this time I win because he's stuck in a loveless marriage, and…"

Tom flinched as if someone had hit him, but responded with a grin. "And what?"

"Nothing."

"Well, we all have our crosses to bear, but at least I still have her."

Marjorie had had enough of the childish battle. "Where is your wife, by the way, Tom? Annette, isn't it?"

"Yes. She's gone to our room to change her dress; she spilt red wine over the front during dinner."

"I must chat to her when she gets back; I haven't met everyone properly just yet."

"Good luck with that," said Wilfred. "Annette doesn't do chats; she only does conflict. Isn't that right, Tom?" Wilfred's triumphant tone was annoying Marjorie. If anyone was argumentative and not just a little bitter, it seemed to be him.

"*My* wife's not comfortable with strangers." Emphasis on my, Marjorie noticed.

Wilfred snorted as he squeezed his cousin's shoulder. "Or with friends, for that matter, especially your female friends." Turning to Marjorie, he added, "Tom's not a one-woman man, if you know what I mean."

Tom's ears reddened. As he brushed his long locks behind them, he gritted his teeth.

"You've had too much to drink, Wilf. You should slow it down."

The men were becoming confrontational again. Marjorie felt it was time to move the subject along once more.

"I haven't seen your mother for a while, Tom. Is she around?"

Tom searched the room with his eyes. Drawing his bushy eyebrows together, he replied, "I didn't notice her leave. Perhaps she's gone to change. She said her shoes were uncomfortable. Mother's got a bit of arthritis in her ankles, but don't tell her I told you; she likes to think she's still in her thirties."

"Don't we all." Marjorie grinned, pleased the tension from a few moments ago had disappeared.

"Maybe she's gone to put your grandma's jewels in a safe." Wilfred clearly couldn't resist having another dig. How these two were ever friends was beyond Marjorie.

Tom's face was taut. His temple pulsated as he again flicked his hair back behind his ears.

"I hope she has, she shouldn't be wearing them."

"I noticed the necklace," said Marjorie. "Rather beautiful, and earrings to match. I'd be worried sick wearing something so obviously valuable. Were they a gift from your grandmother?"

Wilfred laughed, a contorted, sarcastic smirk filling his face. *He really is a most disagreeable man,* thought Marjorie. Tom rubbed his neck, unbuttoning his loud shirt at the collar. He was sweating slightly.

"No, at least I don't think so. Wilf's right. The gems belong to my grandma on my father's side, but I don't know how Mum got hold of them. Perhaps she borrowed them for the anniversary."

"Without the old girl knowing, eh, Tom?" Wilfred nudged his cousin roughly.

"Grandma Elrod's ninety-eight and has a live-in carer because she's not so mobile these days." Tom glared at Wilfred. "She's got all her marbles, though, so not as easily taken advantage of as *Wilf* thinks." His eyes softened as he spoke fondly of his grandmother.

"Maybe not so sharp as you think, either. The old dear's going senile," Wilfred told Marjorie. "I hear she's much more forgetful now, he just doesn't want to admit it. Looks to me like part of your inheritance has gone the way of your parents." Wilfred slurred as he turned his skinny high cheek boned face towards Tom. "Tom's grandma, Grandma Elrod's the one with all the money, isn't that right? She's not always been too fond of her brown-eyed boy's parents, so promised the bulk of the dosh to Thomas, as she calls him. It comes with certain conditions, though."

"Oh, do shut up, *Wilf.* What's it to you, anyway? I'm sure Lady Marjorie doesn't want to hear your opinions on the skeletons in my family's cupboard." Tom turned back to Marjorie. "Grandma Elrod's always been a little on the eccentric side. Now she's vulnerable to vultures." He glared at Wilfred, "I try to protect her. We're close, that's all."

"More like you try to protect your future," muttered Wilfred, just loud enough to be heard.

"Wouldn't she be a Fanston as your father's mother?" Marjorie quizzed, ignoring the annoying Wilfred.

"After she divorced her husband thirty-odd years ago, she went back to using her maiden name. She won't use her title either."

"Tommy here also changed his surname, just to keep in her good books. Eh, Thomas?"

"You should go get some coffee, you're embarrassing yourself," snapped Tom.

"I think I'd prefer to talk to the ladies." Wilfred leered in Rachel and Octavia's direction.

"Give it up, Wilf."

"She's quite a beauty you've got with you, Lady Snellthorpe." Wilfred's eyes bulged, making them look even more lecherous.

"Rachel is a happily married woman and you'll have me to answer to if you upset or offend her in any way. Do you understand, young man?"

Marjorie's sharp tone hit the spot. Wilfred's eyes shot to the floor. He held his palms up in surrender.

"Okay. I was just joking."

Tom chuckled, clearly pleased to see his cousin put in his place.

"I'll chat to Octavia, then, we seemed to get on earlier." Wilfred left them, with Marjorie glaring furiously at his back.

"Don't mind him, he's all mouth," said Tom.

"Does he realise Octavia is my daughter-in-law and my son is in the room? At least, he was." Marjorie glanced around. Annette Elrod had returned, but now Jeremy was gone, as was Lord Fanston. *No doubt hatching their business plan.*

"When he's been on the demon drink, it's hard to know what he realises, Lady Marjorie. I apologise for my cousin's behaviour. He can be quite different when he's sober, but I'm afraid that's a rarity these days. He's resentful and spiteful a lot of the time."

"How sad. Can't he get help for the drinking?"

"Aunt Melody's tried to get him to go into a rehab centre, but he denies having a problem. He hasn't got to the stage of saying, 'I'm Wilfred and I'm an alcoholic' just yet."

"And is he an alcoholic?"

"Who knows? I'm no expert on addiction, but if he's not there yet, he soon will be. I wouldn't pay too much attention to anything he says, though. He mixes fact with the fiction in his head. He's never forgiven me for marrying Annette."

"Surely he's not still in love with your wife?"

Tom stroked his chin slowly, eyes creased. "You know, perhaps you've hit the nail on the head, Lady Marjorie. That would explain a lot of things. We were good friends until I married Annette. I thought he'd got over it, but maybe he never will. It's not true what he said about me and Annette. We're happy enough, but we live our own lives."

"Is your grandfather still alive?"

"No. I saw little of Grandpa when he was alive. He died about ten years ago."

"Do you see much of your grandmother?"

"Yes, she lives a couple of miles away from us. That's one reason we moved to Lincolnshire: so I could be close by in case she needs me."

"Is Wilfred right about her going senile?"

"Not at all. Yes, she's more forgetful these days, but she still knows what's what. At least, I thought she did."

"Do you think she gave the diamonds to your mother?"

Tom bristled. "I doubt it. Unless she gave them to my father and he gave them to Mother. The carer told me my parents visited the day before the cruise." Tom's face darkened. "I wonder if…"

"If what?" asked Marjorie.

"Oh, nothing. By the way, your son's back over there. Perhaps you'd better warn him to keep his wife away from my cousin." Tom nodded his head towards a table where Jeremy was now having a drink with Wilfred's mother, Melody Vanmeter. Marjorie noticed Lord Fanston enter through a door on the far side of the room, looking agitated. He went straight to the bar.

"I don't think there's any danger of Octavia falling for Wilfred's charms," Marjorie tried to sound more certain than she felt. "Now, if you'll excuse me, I'd better check on my friend. I see she's on her own." Wilfred and Octavia were engaged in another flirting session and Rachel had clearly left them to it.

"Good talking to you, Lady Marjorie," Tom gave her a genuine smile. "I'm much more relaxed in older people's company; I hope you don't find that offensive."

"Not at all," she said, walking away thinking, *and with women in general, by the sounds of it.*

Chapter 7

Rachel was relieved to see Marjorie heading in her direction. Jeremy had just come back into the lounge, having been away for the whole time she'd been with Octavia. Lady Fanston had also disappeared early on and hadn't yet returned.

"How did you get on?" Marjorie asked.

"Not very well. I was just getting somewhere when foxy Wilf arrived; he's totally wasted, by the way. I got as far as finding out Octavia knows what Jeremy and Lord Fanston are concocting before we were interrupted. What about you?"

"Nothing on the business front, but there's an awful lot of tension between the two cousins. Wilfred – he doesn't like being called Wilf – is a nasty sort, twisted with it. Tom says it's the drink, but I'm not so sure. Apparently, he was in love with Tom's wife before they were married."

"Unrequited love? And they say a woman spurned is bad."

"Not nearly so bad as a man spurned. Where is the beastly Wilfred, anyway? He was here a moment ago, flirting with my daughter-in-law."

Rachel had observed Octavia and Wilfred for a few moments after Marjorie joined her. "He went out that way," she nodded towards the far door.

"And Octavia?"

"She left just before him, that way," she nodded at a different exit. "I think they argued. Perhaps he went too far."

"Or they wanted it to appear that way."

Rachel shook her head. "I don't think so. Besides, Octavia probably only went to use the toilet. She's been knocking the drink back a bit too."

"My daughter-in-law will always make the most of anything that's free. At least she left through the other door, which is something. I dislike the woman immensely, but I would hate to see Jeremy hurt."

Rachel didn't believe Jeremy had noticed anything amiss; he was so engrossed with whatever was going on between him and Lord Fanston. Perhaps the marriage was already over.

"Jeremy's on his own now. Melody Vanmeter has just headed out as well."

"It's like a train station. Shall we just go? I'm not sure I can take much more socialising with these people. I do like

Tom, although if Wilfred's vitriol is to be believed, he's in a loveless marriage. He is also unfaithful and a womaniser."

"From what I've seen, Wilfred was talking about himself rather than Tom. He hasn't stopped making advances all evening; he gives me the creeps."

"I found out something interesting that I didn't know before," said Marjorie. "Apparently, Lord Fanston's mother is extremely wealthy, but not close to him or Colleen Fanston. Also – and this came from Wilfred, although Tom didn't deny it – she's promised Tom the inheritance. Take this next part with a pinch of caution as it came from Wilfred as well – according to him, the inheritance comes with conditions."

"What conditions?"

"I didn't get to hear the details, but apparently the diamonds belong, or at least belonged to Mrs Elrod. She refuses to use her title."

"Annette?"

"No, dear. Lord Fanston's mother goes by her maiden name, Elrod."

"Now it makes sense why Tom goes by a different surname. Do you think that's one of the conditions?"

"Possibly. Colleen's been gone a long time, hasn't she? I'm surprised she's not holding court."

"Tom's gone as well now, probably to find her."

"Decorum dictates I should at least thank her for the invitation before we leave. Shall we get a drink?"

"Now you're talking. Are we going to join Jeremy? He's looking a bit sulky."

"Not yet. I need a brandy before I speak to my son. I would also like to take the weight off my legs for a moment. Do you mind if I sit down? There's a quiet table over there."

"Not at all. The waiters are busy, I'll go to the bar."

After making sure Marjorie was sitting comfortably and that she was all right, Rachel approached the bar. At the opposite end, Lord Fanston was sitting on a barstool. He still appeared flustered. Was it because Jeremy hadn't managed to get his mother to play ball so far? Rachel was worried about Marjorie; she was strong, but there was no doubt Jeremy's announcement earlier had affected her.

"What can I get you, ma'am?"

"A large brandy and a martini and lemonade, please."

The young bartender returned moments later with the two drinks. Rachel offered her cruise payment card.

"Compliments of the gentleman down there," the woman said. Rachel turned her head to see Jeremy had joined Lord Fanston. He gave her a nod and a smile. She mouthed a thank you and took the drinks over to Marjorie.

"Courtesy of Jeremy," she said.

"Peace offering, I expect. At least that's a start."

Rachel had hoped the tension created by Jeremy's earlier revelation would dissipate, but she was pretty sure that would only happen if they didn't have to see too much of the Fanston party.

Captain Jenson reappeared while they were enjoying their drinks and ushered all the Fanstons' guests back into the room where they had eaten dinner. They had placed a table in the centre of the room and a chef appeared, wheeling a huge anniversary cake. Champagne corks were popping in the background as the waiters prepared for what was obviously going to be the formal congratulatory announcement.

Captain Jenson checked his watch and looked at Tatum Rodman, the assistant cruise director, who was standing ready with her microphone. She shrugged her shoulders, shaking her head, then went over to speak to Lord Fanston. After they'd had a brief conversation, Tatum returned to the captain, clearly explaining what was happening.

Rachel and Marjorie took their drinks to a free table, both watching the unravelling scene.

"Oh dear. It appears Lady Fanston wants to keep everyone waiting once more. She does like to make an entrance, doesn't she?" Marjorie remarked.

"Bordering on rude, if you ask me," said Rachel.

"She's a wannabe, Rachel, nothing more, nothing less. If I were Captain Jenson, I'd leave."

"He's as polite as you are, Marjorie. Aren't we still here because of your etiquette?"

"Touché."

"All the others are here at least, so we can leave after the formal congratulations are over," Rachel said hopefully.

"Except for Tom, he's not back yet. You're right, he must have gone to find his mother."

Rachel's eyes scanned the waiting party of people. Again, she detected the smouldering conflict lying just beneath the surface of the false smiles and extravagant gestures. She felt tension in her neck; too much time had passed for Lady Fanston to be intending to make a late entrance.

The doors, which had been closed, suddenly burst open and they could hear once more the sound of the music and dancing from the other room. Rachel's worst fears were confirmed as Tom came rushing into the room.

"My mother's missing. Dad, she's not here, and she's not in your room. I found these on the suite balcony." Tom held up the blue evening bag Lady Fanston had been carrying all evening and the shawl that had been over her shoulders.

***

Captain Jenson moved to close the doors to the function room as the small crowd gathered around the distraught-looking Tom. Rachel and Marjorie exchanged a worried glance as they listened in.

"Of course she's not missing. You know your mother – she's probably gone off for a late-night shop," Lord Fanston said firmly, although he was rubbing his hands through his hair, showing the same signs of agitation he had been displaying since returning to the party.

"No, Dad. I'm telling you, she's gone. There's a broken champagne glass on the balcony and an opened bottle still on the table. I think she might have fallen overboard."

"Take some deep breaths, Mr Elrod," Captain Jenson instructed. Turning to Lord Fanston, he asked, "How long since your wife left the party?"

"I couldn't tell you, I was talking with Jeremy Snellthorpe all evening."

"She left about an hour and a half ago," Jeremy chipped in. "Don't you remember, Harvey? She said we were boring her with business talk and she was going to change her shoes, something about the slingback digging into her heel. Whatever that means."

"Oh yes, now I remember. Annette left a few minutes later, Tom."

Rachel couldn't help thinking she was watching a scene from a play where everyone knew their lines.

Turning to Annette Elrod, Lord Fanston quizzed, "Did you see my wife?"

Annette appeared uncomfortable as all eyes moved in her direction.

"No, I didn't. I spilt wine on my dress, so I left to change."

"But you're wearing the same dress, aren't you?" Octavia quizzed, gleefully.

"Erm… yes, I am. I went to the restroom and managed to get most of the wine out, so I changed my mind and came back here. Why are you all looking at me like that? I didn't see Colleen."

"So you say, but who knows? For all we know, you could have followed her." Octavia chortled and Marjorie glared at her inappropriate daughter-in-law. Jeremy drew his wife aside, having a word.

Captain Jenson intervened. "May I remind everyone that this is no laughing matter and we don't need to suggest anything untoward has happened. Lady Fanston is missing at present. This is a big ship and she could have gone anywhere. Is her cruise card still in the purse?"

Lord Fanston snatched the evening bag from Tom and looked inside.

"No, it's not."

"There we have it." The captain sounded relieved. "If Lady Fanston took it with her, Lord Fanston might be quite right in assuming his wife went somewhere else."

"Not to the shops," said Tatum. "They closed forty minutes ago. I've called for Chief Waverley; he's on his way, sir."

"Shouldn't we stop the ship and put out a man overboard signal?" Tom's eyes widened. "Woman overboard. You know what I mean."

"Indeed I do, Mr Elrod, but we can't do that every time a passenger wanders off, I'm afraid," said Captain Jenson. "In ninety-nine per cent of cases, people lose track of time and turn up later. And without evidence to the contrary and with her cruise card not being in her handbag… well, it makes it unlikely anything odd has happened. Now, Mr Elrod, please tell us exactly what occurred tonight."

The look on the captain's face said it all. If Lady Fanston had gone over the side, they would have no chance of finding her at night and she would have no chance of surviving a fall into the freezing cold Atlantic Ocean.

Marjorie nudged Rachel, whispering, "I don't like the look of this."

Rachel whispered, "Me neither," then turned her attention back to listen to Tom.

"I noticed Mother had been gone a long time and was worried about the way she'd been knocking back the booze. She's not used to it, unlike some," he said, glowering pointedly at Wilfred before continuing. "I asked a lady to check the restroom outside, but there was no-one in there fitting my mother's description. Then I thought she might have gone back to her suite for something and fallen asleep – she does that sometimes – but when I went inside, she wasn't there—"

"How did you get in, then?" quizzed Wilfred, who seemed remarkably sober all of a sudden.

"The door was open."

"That's not possible! All the doors are spring-locked," Wilfred challenged.

Tom flicked the hair back from his forehead and tucked the length behind his reddening ears. "Something was jammed in it, holding it ajar. Anyway, the balcony doors were open, so I went outside to check. That's when I saw the broken glass and the items I brought back with me."

"Why did you come straight back here," Lord Fanston snapped at his son, "rather than looking for your mother?"

"I didn't!" Tom snapped back. "I looked over the side, but it was all black. I couldn't see a thing, and it was so cold…" Tom paused, eyes darting around. "I checked the bedroom, the bathroom and the corridor, then I feared the worst."

"Was there any sign of the diamond necklace and earrings?"

Rachel had wondered who would be the first to ask about the gems. It was Octavia.

"What? Oh, those. I didn't look."

"Of course you did," snorted Wilfred. "You picked up a handbag and a shawl, but didn't notice whether million-pound diamonds were lying around?"

"Look, you," Tom grabbed Wilfred's jacket collars and dragged him close, snarling, "My mother is missing, so jewels weren't on my priority list. If she's gone overboard, we should assume they went with her."

Wilfred struggled free. "Or not," he sneered.

"Gentlemen, please." Again, Captain Jenson intervened. "Calm down, this is not helping. We'll call guest services and put out a ship-wide announcement requesting Lady Fanston join us here. Tatum, you go down to reception in case she turns up there."

"Yes, sir."

"Ah, here's a person who should be able to help."

Jack Waverley joined the group, his face red from the effort of rushing from wherever he had been when he got the call. He nodded a greeting to Rachel and Marjorie. Marjorie smirked. Rachel nudged her.

"Behave."

"This is our head of security, Chief Waverley." Captain Jenson introduced the guests and explained briefly to Waverley what had happened so far.

"I'm telling you, we should stop the ship," yelled Tom.

"With your permission, Lord Fanston, I'd like to have one of my security team go to your suite." Waverley ignored the emotional Tom, who was led to a seat by Melody Vanmeter.

"Yes, of course. I think I'll go up there myself if that's all right? I want to see if she left a note telling us where she's gone. I'm sure there's a simple explanation."

Waverley hesitated. "Yes, sir, you may go, but please don't disturb anything until my officer joins you." He turned away and spoke into his radio. "Inglis, we may have a missing passenger. Please check and search the Royal Suite. Lady Colleen Fanston, you'll find her details on the passenger list. Her husband's on the way up. She's aged seventy-nine…"

A voice crackled back through the radio. "What would she be wearing, sir?"

"Just a minute." Waverley turned to Rachel as the others were all talking at once, exchanging theories.

"A sea-blue dress with matching sandals and," she lowered her voice, "a million-pound diamond necklace with matching earrings."

Waverley's forehead wrinkled as he repeated the information into the radio, moving further away from the group when he mentioned the diamonds. Rachel couldn't hear the response. The chief shook his head, most likely pondering the same theory as Rachel. Was this a wandering septuagenarian, or an aggravated robbery, and if the latter, where was Lady Colleen Fanston?

Chapter 8

Before Waverley started interviewing the guests, Rachel drew him to one side.

"Marjorie's tired. I think I should take her to her room. Can you speak to us later?"

Waverley ran a hand through his thinning hair, his eyes scrunched, showing stress. "Yes, of course. You know where to find me if I'm not here when you come back. Do you know if this disappearing act is out of character for Lady Fanston?"

"Sorry, I only met her tonight. I understand she likes to make an entrance; she was a little late for dinner, but this appears to go well beyond that."

"Quite. I do hope we find the woman soon."

"Me too," said Rachel.

Marjorie raised an eyebrow when she returned. "What was that all about?"

"I asked if I could take you back to your room."

"Not on your life!"

"We don't have to go back, but I'd rather we talk in private."

Marjorie tapped her nose. "Why didn't you say so? Come on, let's go to mission headquarters."

Rachel assumed Marjorie meant the Jazz Bar, where they had met frequently in the past to discuss cases. "Actually, I have somewhere else in mind." She took her friend's arm.

"You do?"

"Shh, Jeremy's coming over."

"Mother, are you all right? Dreadful business, but don't worry, I'm sure they'll find her. I've just told the chief she likes blackjack and could be in the casino."

"Let's hope so. I'm quite well, but I'm rather tired, Jeremy. I think I'll go to bed. Rachel will see me safely back to my room."

"Thank you, Rachel. I'm just waiting for Tom so we can go and help with the search. The chief's finished with me; I'll let Octavia know where I'm going." He glanced over at his wife, who was giggling like a schoolchild at something Wilfred Vanmeter was saying. Jeremy frowned.

"Yes, you do that. I suspect she'll have a thumping headache in the morning. By the way, where did you go this evening?"

"What do you mean? I've been here the whole time." A bead of sweat formed on Jeremy's brow under his mother's piercing gaze. "Oh, you mean when I went to the gents?"

Rather a long visit to the gents, Rachel thought, but didn't comment.

"That must have been it. I was hoping for a chat, but never mind. Tomorrow will do." Marjorie turned to leave.

"I'll take care of her," Rachel assured the bemused Jeremy.

"Right." He turned abruptly. Rachel wished he wasn't so much like his mother at times; they were both stubborn and self-willed, neither giving an inch.

Once they were in the corridor, Marjorie looked up at her.

"Where to, Sherlock?"

Rachel squeezed her arm. "You're as bad as Sarah sometimes with your teasing. I thought we would go and check on Lord Fanston to see if he's okay."

"Ahh, now I understand. Good plan. I know the way to the Royal Suite; Ralph and I stayed there for our diamond wedding anniversary celebrations, too. I do wish Jeremy had turned out more like his father."

"We are who we are, Marjorie. Jeremy loves you, that's the most important thing."

Marjorie patted Rachel's hand. "You're right, dear. I believe he does, underneath all the bluster. Now, let's go and see what's happened to that troublesome woman. It will be no surprise to me if she has staged her own disappearance for attention."

"Surely not!" exclaimed Rachel.

"You're quite right. Who would do such a thing? It's been an odd evening all round, if you ask me. People in and out of the room like they're on a conveyor belt, secret chit-chats, and Colleen Fanston disappearing from her own party. It's hardly the thing to do, is it?"

Rachel pondered as they walked, taking the lift to the seventeenth deck where they had to wait outside the locked door which led into the Royal Suite corridor.

"We'll need to tailgate someone as they go in," she said.

"What on earth does that entail?"

"You'll see. Follow my lead. Here's a crewman now. If he queries our presence, feign dizziness or something."

"Now that I can do," Marjorie chuckled.

The crewman unlocked the door with a swipe card, and Rachel arrived at his back. "Here, let me." She held the door so the man could get the large circular tray and his slight frame through.

"Thank you, ma'am," the waiter said, continuing on his way. Rachel carried on holding the door, allowing Marjorie through.

"That was easy," said Marjorie. "It helped that the tray was bigger than he was, I suppose." Rachel laughed.

They had entered a wide corridor in an interior part of the ship she had never seen before. Plush carpet lined the floor and scenic pictures adorned the mocha-coloured walls.

"That's a Hockney," said Marjorie, stopping to admire a large, framed picture.

"Not a real one?" Rachel gawped.

"Hardly. Even Queen Cruises' penchant for elaborate decor wouldn't stretch that far. Too tempting for the many art thieves who like to cruise."

"Now you're having me on."

"I certainly am not!" Marjorie's chin jutted forward.

Rachel held her palms up in surrender. "Okay, a story for another day. Where's the Royal Suite?"

"Follow me," said Marjorie, heading along the lengthy corridor in the direction the crewman had taken. They stopped at a T-junction with windows overlooking a well-lit private swimming pool, Jacuzzi and spa rooms with their own bar.

"Is that all for the Royal Suite?" Rachel asked.

"It's shared with the owned suites, although the owners only ever use them for a few months a year. When we were here, we had the pool to ourselves. Ralph loved an early morning dip; it's heated in the winter. Can you see the Jacuzzi on the far side?"

"I can. What's in the spa rooms?"

"There's a sauna in one and steam room in the other."

"Lady Fanston wouldn't be out there, would she?"

"I doubt it, but if she was in the Jacuzzi, you wouldn't see her from here. I can't imagine her taking a sauna instead of going to her own anniversary party. Why don't you go and ask the barman?"

"And say I'm who, exactly? Besides, Security Officer Rosemary Inglis will have checked that first, I'm sure. I met her on the last cruise; she's thorough."

"Unlike some we could mention."

"You need to go easy on Waverley."

Ignoring Rachel's last remark, Marjorie continued. "Well, if you're sure, the Royal is this way. The private suites are on that side." Marjorie turned left and Rachel followed after her. The suite door was closed. There was no noise coming from inside. Rachel knocked. No reply. She knocked again.

"Is there a butler?"

"Yes, they should be in the room we passed. Shall we try there? If it's Glenis, I'm sure she'll remember me."

"How could one forget?" teased Rachel.

They retreated along the corridor and Marjorie knocked on a brown door, oak-stained to match the veneer lining the walls.

"I wouldn't have known this was here without studying hard," said Rachel.

"That's the idea, I think."

The door opened and a sturdy woman with cropped black hair and an unsmiling, heavily made-up face stood before them. She looked questioningly at Rachel before recognising Marjorie.

"Lady Marjorie! What are you doing here?" The woman's friendly tone reassured Rachel. "You came back to see me? I've been wanting to thank you so much for what you did."

Marjorie stood back, appraising the butler.

"It was nothing. I hope everything turned out well."

"Sadly, my grandfather died, but I got to say goodbye. That was the most important thing." Tears welled up in the woman's eyes.

"You're looking well, Glenis."

"I feel well and I've managed to save up enough money, so I'll soon be able to find work on land, I hope. I've got friends in Germany and might move there."

"It will be a tremendous loss to the ship, but I understand. I love the makeup, but the hair needs some work," said Marjorie, chuckling.

Glenis laughed loudly. "You always teased me about my hair. I'll grow it one day and surprise you. How's your husband?"

Marjorie's head drooped, and Glenis clapped her hand to her mouth.

"I'm so sorry. I didn't know. When?"

"Not long after that cruise, actually, but we all have to die, eventually."

"Would you like to come in? It's not as tidy as I'd like; it's been a bit chaotic here. I was glad to see the back of a sheikh this morning, but he gave me a generous tip so I can't complain. Then I had to help with a cocktail party and getting new guests ready for a big party tonight. Now one of them has gone missing."

"We'd love to come in, Glenis. That's the other reason we're here, actually; we were at the party and heard our hostess has gone astray. We wanted to check whether they have found her. This is my dear friend, Rachel Jacobi-Prince."

Glenis opened the door wide, inviting them to enter. "Pleased to meet you, Rachel Jacobi-Prince. Perhaps you could give me some hair tips while you're here. Your hair is gorgeous."

Glenis took a chunk of Rachel's hair in her long fingers and stroked it gently. Rachel felt herself blush, but smiled.

"Thank you."

Glenis did a quick tidy up once they were inside to make enough space for them to sit. "If you haven't guessed, Rachel, Lady Marjorie helped me get home to Russia to visit my sick grandfather. I don't know what I would have done without her and Lord Snellthorpe's help. They persuaded the cruise line to let me go and paid for my tickets."

Rachel had been the recipient of her friend's generosity and knew how Marjorie liked to help people whenever she could. She was proud to know her.

Marjorie nudged the conversation back towards Lady Fanston. "Did you see her after she left for the party, Glenis?"

"No. They said they would be back late and not to wait up. I turned the beds down, took some pills for my back, and fell asleep. I didn't wake until a security guard banged the door."

"Did you hear anything before that? Lady Fanston's son said he came looking for her," Rachel quizzed.

"Sorry, no. The tablets and working a long day knocked me out; I didn't hear nothing."

"Anything, dear."

Glenis looked confused.

"If you're going to be a young lady," explained Marjorie, "your diction needs improving. You say I didn't hear *anything*."

"I think that's language rather than diction," said Rachel protectively as Glenis appeared hurt.

Marjorie burst out laughing, and Glenis joined in. "You're teasing me again. She always did this to me when her and her husband came on the cruise. She called me yob, and I called her snob."

Rachel liked the interaction between Marjorie and the butler and wondered why Marjorie had never mentioned Glenis before.

"Did you notice anything keeping the door to the suite open?" Rachel returned to her questioning.

"No. The door was locked after the Fanstons left for the evening. I checked."

"If Lady Fanston had returned and was expecting somebody, could she have left something to prop the door open?"

"It's possible," Glenis admitted.

"How would they get through the outer doors?" Rachel persisted.

"Lady Fanston could have opened them," Marjorie suggested.

"But then there would have been no need to leave anything in the door," said Rachel.

"Unless it was the outer door Tom was referring to," Marjorie argued.

"You've lost me," said Glenis.

Rachel rubbed her temples. "We'll park that one for now. Do you know what the security officer found?"

Glenis shook her head. "No. She spoke to the pool attendant and barman outside, asked me to look around the suite to see if anything was different, and then told me to leave her to it. Lord Fanston arrived when I was leaving."

"And was anything different?" Rachel asked.

"The balcony doors were wide open; it was like fridge in there. There was a champagne bottle on the table and a broken glass on the floor. I offered to clear it away, but was told not to. Lord Fanston knocked a short while later and told me to clear it away. I replaced the glasses."

"Glasses, you say? Where was the other one?"

"I don't know. Both glasses were there when I turned the bed down, next to champagne bucket, but later one was broken and one had disappeared. Maybe she dropped it over the side."

"Interesting," said Rachel. "Do you happen to know where Lord Fanston is now?"

"I thought he was in his room. Maybe he went looking for wife."

"Would you mind opening the door for us and checking whether he's in? I won't get a wink of sleep unless I know Colleen's safe," said Marjorie.

"For you, Lady Marjorie, anything."

Glenis sprang up, opened her door, and trotted down the corridor. Rachel pursued her and Marjorie followed more slowly. The butler knocked at the door first and waited a few moments. When there was no reply, she unlocked it. The lights were still on, but nobody was in the room. A draught of cold air hit them, but the balcony doors were firmly shut.

"Lord Fanston!" Glenis called. No reply.

Marjorie shuffled past the butler and marched through the room, heading straight to the balcony doors. Rachel joined her and they peered through. Glenis flicked a switch to turn on the balcony light. It was huge; Rachel's was big in her luxury suite on deck fifteen, but this was almost big enough to hold an outdoor dinner party.

"Oh dear, Glenis, I think you missed a bit of glass over there," remarked Marjorie, pointing past the large sun loungers and table which had four chairs neatly tucked underneath.

Glenis stiffened. "Where?"

"Just down there," Marjorie pointed to the far corner. Rachel couldn't see anything.

Glenis opened the balcony door to go outside. The night chill blew through into the room, but the butler pulled the door closed, leaving just a small gap open.

Marjorie inclined her head to Rachel. "Check the bedroom. I'll keep her busy."

"I can't find it," Rachel heard Glenis say as she sneaked into the couple's bedroom for a quick scan, keeping half an ear open for Marjorie's warning that the butler might be finished on her wild goose chase.

"I'm sure I saw it. Perhaps it's in the gutter. I do think you should look."

Rachel grinned. Her shrewd friend could convince anyone to do anything when she had a mind to, as Rachel had discovered since getting to know her.

The distraction wasn't much help, however, because there was nothing to be found in the bedroom within the short time she had to look around. Two large suitcases had been unpacked and stored away neatly in a wardrobe large enough to house a family's clothes for a year, let alone a couple's for a few weeks. The beds had been turned down as Glenis described, and a slab of luxury chocolate with tomorrow's *Coral News* lay on top of each. Neatly folded pyjamas lay on the bed nearest the door and a nightdress on the other. If Lady Fanston had returned to her room, it didn't look like she'd been in here.

Hearing Marjorie still yelling instructions as to where the imaginary shard of glass could be, Rachel took a quick peek inside the luxury bathroom before returning to the sitting room.

Chapter 9

"Did you find anything?" Marjorie quizzed as soon as they left the private corridor and arrived on the communal part of deck seventeen again.

Rachel shook her head. "Nothing, other than the Fanstons sleep in separate beds."

"A lot of older people sleep in separate beds. It doesn't mean there's anything wrong with the marriage."

"I agree," said Rachel. "So we're no wiser. Did you get anything else out of Glenis?"

"I'm afraid not. She must have slept through whatever happened, which is most unhelpful. I wonder if there's CCTV?"

"I couldn't see any cameras in the corridors, but Waverley would know better. I'm sure, he told me once, they have cameras scanning the ship's sides, so if she did go overboard, they should know about it by now. He's bound to have someone checking that footage."

"Why didn't Waverley mention that when he was in the function room?"

"It would hardly be the first thing he'd declare to a distraught family, would it?"

"I suppose not, but I have a bad feeling about this, Rachel. Colleen Fanston doesn't strike me as one to leave her own party in the first place. From what I've seen and heard of her, she enjoys being the centre of attention."

"You think someone lured her away?"

"Don't you?"

"It's possible, and a clandestine meeting would explain why she left her door jammed open if she did. But how would the person get through the outer door? I don't think she'd have propped that one open, not with crew going in and out."

"Someone is staying in one of the residents' suites. That waiter we saw headed that way, didn't he?"

"Yes, we need to find out who, just in case they saw anything."

"I do hope scruffy Tom is telling the truth, and he hasn't done anything stupid."

Rachel shuddered in the cold; she hadn't brought a shawl. "Come on. Let's get back indoors. It's time to catch up with Waverley."

They made their way quietly back to the function room, each lost in her own thoughts. Rachel was working hard to form a mental picture of at what point and in which order each person left the room, and how long they were gone. If something had happened to Lady Fanston, she was convinced it wouldn't have been an accident, and that one or more members of their party knew exactly what had occurred. Although the million-pound necklace and diamond earrings would be incentive enough to attract an opportunist to take a chance on robbery, it remained more likely it was someone Lady Fanston knew.

"You think she's been murdered, don't you?" Marjorie's question broke through her musings.

"I don't believe she accidentally fell over the side, if that is what happened. The rails are too high for starters. She would have had to climb on a chair and leap over."

"You make a good point there. What if she committed suicide?"

"If she's dead, and we don't know yet whether she is, suicide would be one line of enquiry, I'm sure. But if Glenis is right, someone else could have been in that room. Otherwise, the other champagne glass would have been in its place."

"Perhaps the security officer took it; they could be sweeping it for prints."

"I'm surprised they didn't sweep the whole balcony for prints, to be honest. Why let Lord Fanston call Glenis to clean up?"

"Another good point. Perhaps they've found the silly woman after all."

Rachel and Marjorie re-entered the dining room off the function room. It was empty. The anniversary cake remained centre stage on the table, untouched. A model of a happy couple stood on the top and gold ribbon decorated the lower tier.

"Brings it home, doesn't it?" Marjorie said quietly.

"Yes, it does. Some celebration…"

They stood for a few moments, again lost in their own thoughts. The party was still going on in the larger function room.

"Come on, Marjorie. Let's go." Rachel scanned the dance floor as they passed through and noticed Wilfred dancing with a woman they hadn't met. She paused. "Who's that with Wilfred?" she asked.

"Goodness me, he doesn't let the grass grow under his feet, does he? Shall I interrupt them?"

Rachel watched Wilfred falling about the dance floor, making a complete idiot of himself. "It's not worth it. I don't think we'll get much sense out of him tonight. Let's go and speak to Waverley."

"Do we have to?" Marjorie sighed.

"Or you could go to your room, save me explaining why you're still up."

"Sarcasm doesn't become you, Rachel. I'm coming with you, but I can't promise to be patient with him if he's going to behave like a buffoon."

"You make him nervous. Give him a break."

"Humph. He needs to grow some backbone."

The chief's light was on and Rachel recognised Rosemary Inglis, the ex-Olympian security officer who she'd met on the previous cruise. She felt relieved. If someone else was there, Marjorie might go easier on the security chief.

She knocked on the door. Waverley looked up from his desk, surprised. He motioned for them to go in.

"Marjorie couldn't sleep for worrying about Lady Fanston," Rachel said, which was partly true. "Have you found her?"

Rosemary grinned at the two of them.

"Don't play games with me, Rachel," the chief replied. "Good evening, Lady Snellthorpe." He held his hand up. "Before you dig yourself in any deeper, Inglis here has just informed me where you've both been."

"Guilty as charged, but we only went because Marjorie was worried," Rachel persisted. "I presume Glenis told you?"

Rosemary nodded. "I went back to gather evidence and dust for prints."

"But the champagne glass had been cleared away," Rachel said.

Waverley's face went purple. "If he wasn't a lord staying in the Royal Suite with a missing wife, I'd…"

Lady Marjorie chuckled. "You'd what, Chief?"

"I couldn't possibly say in front of you ladies."

"It most likely wouldn't have helped us anyway," said Rosemary. "The butler tells me they had people for drinks in the suite after boarding. There would be prints all over the place."

"So, what did you two find out?" Waverley quizzed.

Rachel puffed out her cheeks and blew out a disappointed breath. "Absolutely nothing, other than what you already know. Lord Fanston asked the butler to clear away the mess on the balcony. The only thing worth adding is there was another champagne glass, and it's missing, unless you have it?" She looked at Rosemary, who shook her head.

"Not much to go on, is it?" Waverley moaned.

"Did you find out anything?"

"Alas, we have to fear the worst. Lady Fanston is nowhere to be found on board the *Coral*. We've alerted ships in the area and the coastguard. We have to assume she either fell or, more likely, jumped overboard. Contrary to popular opinion, it's hard to fall over the side of a cruise ship."

"Hard, but not impossible, Chief," said Marjorie.

"Quite."

"Do you have any CCTV footage?" Rachel asked.

Waverley's neck and face turned a dark shade of beetroot. She noticed the tremor in his right hand – the one she'd seen on the previous cruise – as he rubbed his hand through his hair and emitted his habitual nervous cough.

"No."

"Why ever not?" Marjorie snapped.

"It seems some idiot disconnected the lead from the mainframe in the security hub by mistake. A cleaner, most likely, being overenthusiastic with the duster."

Rachel nudged Marjorie not to say anything.

"How much of a gap is there?"

Waverley looked down at his hands.

"Six hours, thirty-five minutes. I found the lead disconnected when I went to check the timeframe," Rosemary answered. She looked sheepishly towards Waverley. "There's been a loose lead problem for a while; it hasn't been replaced because we're getting a completely new surveillance system soon. We all check it's in place whenever we're in the hub, but we missed the check today."

"Speaking of which, where is that blasted Ravanos? It's not the first time he's forgotten."

Rachel had met Ravanos, a gentle security officer on Waverley's team, in the past. He wasn't the brainiest, but was very willing. Easily duped, he often ended up in the chief's bad books.

"He's typing up statements, sir."

"We've not been introduced," Lady Marjorie said to Rosemary.

"I do apologise," Waverley snapped out of the doldrums. "Lady Marjorie, this is Rosemary Inglis; she joined us last year. She's my right hand, erm… person since Goodridge went on leave."

"Pleased to meet you." Lady Marjorie held out her hand.

Rosemary shook it. "I've heard all about you from Jason and Sarah."

"And you've met Rachel, I take it?"

"Yeah. We met on the New Year cruise. Quite eventful if I remember right."

"She does tend to bring trouble wherever she goes," laughed Marjorie.

"Pot calling kettle black comes to mind, and that time the trouble was already here. That's why I was called," Rachel quipped back.

Waverley's heavy sigh cut through the laughter like a knife. "I hate to remind you three, but I have a missing person to find."

"I thought you said she was nowhere to be found?" Marjorie challenged.

"Investigate, then. I have a missing person to investigate."

"Did anyone actually see Lady Fanston return to her room, or are we just assuming she did?" Rachel asked.

"We don't have anyone who actually saw her, but Thomas Elrod, her son, said he found the champagne and a broken glass on the balcony," Waverley said.

"Don't you find it odd that a skinny seventy-nine-year-old was sitting out on an ice-cold balcony supping champagne?" Rachel asked. "Glenis said the room was freezing."

"Who the heck's Glenis?" Waverley snapped.

"The butler, sir, and she's right: it was extremely cold in there."

"Are you suggesting someone staged the woman being outside?" Waverley quizzed.

"I just find it difficult to imagine the woman I met tonight sitting on her sub-zero balcony instead of being at her own diamond wedding anniversary party, that's all."

"But Mr Elrod found her bag and her shawl out there," Waverley argued.

"So he says," commented Rachel.

"I like that young man and he seemed so distressed when he came back," Marjorie said.

"I'm not saying he's not telling the truth, but we have to think of all possibilities. So far, we only have his word to back up the theory that his mother may have gone over the balcony. He seemed pretty peeved about her turning up to the party wearing the diamonds. Didn't Wilfred tell you they were meant to be Tom's inheritance? People have killed for less."

"I'm not sure we can take Wilfred's word for anything. Besides, if she was done in, it could have been anyone." Marjorie was becoming agitated. "Every person left the party at some stage during the evening, including Harvey Fanston who would have access to the room."

"He seemed flustered when he got back from wherever it was he went," Rachel conceded.

"Before you two ladies go off on whacky theories, perhaps we should all sit down and you can give us your version of this evening's events," Waverley suggested. Marjorie obliged by taking a seat on the small sofa in the sitting area of Waverley's office. Rachel joined her, while Rosemary sat in a chair. "What can I get you to drink?" Waverley asked.

"A pot of coffee for me," said Rachel. "I've had enough alcohol for one night."

"And for you, Lady Marjorie?"

"A small brandy, please."

"Inglis?" Rosemary looked up, surprised no doubt at the offer of a beverage.

"I'll join Rachel with the coffee, please, sir."

Waverley got on the telephone and requested the coffees before pouring Marjorie a brandy and himself a whisky from his personal supply. They chatted politely while waiting for the coffee to arrive, with Rachel explaining to Marjorie that Rosemary had been a slalom kayaker in the 2012 Olympics.

"That must have been wonderful," said Marjorie, clearly impressed.

Rosemary flushed. "I have wonderful memories, but you can't do stuff like that forever. Besides, I wasn't that good; I didn't win anything outside of the European championships."

"Don't do yourself down," said Marjorie. "Few people can say they were an Olympian. Be proud, my dear."

The coffee arrived, ending Rosemary's awkwardness. Once it was poured, they returned to the subject of the party.

Rachel sat back, deep in thought, while Marjorie explained about the arrival of the glamorous Lady Colleen Fanston to the party and the effect the diamonds appeared to have over the company. She took longer than required, discussing events over dinner, including how charming the captain had been and what she had eaten. Waverley huffed a few times, but soon realised the more he did so, the more elongated Marjorie's account would become. She was never one to miss the opportunity to wind the security chief up.

She also pointed out the underlying tension among those gathered for the party and the odd comings and goings after dinner, neglecting to mention her own son and daughter-in-law's solo exits. Rachel was convinced this was an oversight rather than a deliberate withholding of information, and that Waverley would have already been informed of most of what Marjorie was telling him. No-one appeared to know at what stage Lady Fanston herself had departed or why, except for Jeremy. Rachel thought it odd that Lord Fanston had needed to be reminded of the fact his wife had departed earlier, but all present had imbibed a lot of drink.

"So, if someone followed Lady Fanston, it could have been anyone from the party?" Waverley surmised.

"She wasn't followed," Rachel mused out loud.

"Did you see her leave?" Waverley asked.

"No, but that's the point. She appeared to leave almost secretly, as if she had arranged to meet with someone."

"Who?"

"That's the million dollar – or, in this instance, the million-pound question. If it was the necklace and earrings the secret rendezvous was about, when we find out who she was meeting, we find out what happened to her and the diamonds."

"And what if she was just an unhappily married woman who decided to take her own life? Lady Snellthorpe described her as a woman who liked to make a statement, so perhaps this was her way of saying 'To hell with you all and I'm taking the diamonds with me'," Rosemary suggested.

"The officer makes a good point," said Marjorie. "It would explain why she borrowed, or more likely sneaked, the diamonds away from her mother-in-law and wore them to the party."

"That's the place to start, then," said Rachel. "We dig around into whether the marriage was a good one or a facade, while the security team finds out whether the diamonds were indeed borrowed or stolen. I don't suppose you can get prints from the champagne bottle and glass?"

Rosemary shook her head. "The remains of the glass already went into the recycling, along with hundreds of others. Lord Fanston picked the bottle up when he came in while I was checking the balcony, swore about damned champagne and it being some anniversary before throwing it over the side."

"Did you ask Lord Fanston to leave the room untouched?" quizzed Rachel.

"No, I didn't get the chance. After he threw the bottle over the side, he stomped back inside, checked the safe, muttered something, and left without saying another word."

"Dangerous thing to do. That bottle could have been blown back in and hit someone, not to mention littering the sea," complained Waverley.

"Odd man," said Marjorie. "It appears then, he was more interested in the diamonds than his wife's disappearance."

"He may have been in shock, but then why go back to the suite so quickly, ask for the balcony to be cleaned and throw the bottle over the side? It's not only odd, but downright suspicious," said Rachel. She recalled it was Octavia who had mentioned the diamonds first on hearing about Lady Fanston's disappearance, but didn't want to mention that fact in front of Waverley.

"I'm sure if he'd knocked his wife off, he would have disposed of the bottle at the same time rather than doing it in front of a security officer," said Waverley.

Rachel nodded agreement.

"I'm hoping that if there is a body, it will turn up as the tides wash it in tomorrow or the next day. We can then establish whether the diamonds are on her person, which would support Inglis's theatrical suicide theory. If the diamonds are missing, we may have to consider foul play. We will, of course, continue to scour the ship in case she's fallen somewhere and hasn't been able to summon help. From what we've established, Lady Fanston had a lot to drink before, during, and after dinner. If she returned to her cabin and drank more champagne, she may even have accidentally fallen overboard, no matter how unlikely. As you pointed out, Lady Marjorie, it happens."

"We won't take up any more of your time, Chief. As you say, you've got work to do." Marjorie rose, a pallor appearing on her face as if she had just realised something.

Waverley and Rosemary stood. "Goodnight, Lady Snellthorpe, and thank you for your time," said Waverley.

When they got outside, Marjorie leant into Rachel. "You don't think Jeremy could have anything to do with this awful business, do you?"

Rachel had been wondering when the thought might occur to her friend. She'd hardly dared think it herself, but he would be a suspect, along with everyone else who'd been at the party.

"I think we need to find out about this business proposition, and also whether our invitation came from both Lord and Lady Fanston, or from one of them."

"Why does that matter?"

"Well, if it came from her, she would be unlikely to go off and commit suicide afterwards, surely? If Rosemary's right, it would have been a 'damn you' to the family, not to us. Try not to think about it anymore. You need to get some sleep."

"I fear that's going to be a mission impossible tonight, dear, but I'll give it a shot."

Chapter 10

The telephone on her bedside table letting out a loud, intermittent shrill woke Rachel the next morning. Feeling as though she had only just gone to sleep, she picked it up sleepily, noting the number was that of an unknown stateroom.

"Hello," she sat up, rubbing sleep from her eyes.

"Rachel? It's Jeremy. I can't get hold of Mother. Is she with you?"

Rachel was awake instantly and switched on her bedside light, checking the time: nine-thirty.

"No, she's not. We had a rather late night in the end, she might have slept in. I'll check and get back to you."

"I'm meeting Harvey for breakfast, and I was hoping Mother would join us. Tell her we'll be in the Coral Restaurant, will you?"

Rachel was about to ask after Lady Fanston, but the phone went dead. She dialled Marjorie's room herself, wondering if her friend might be avoiding speaking to her son. The call was answered after a few rings.

"Good morning, Rachel."

"Jeremy's just phoned me."

"Fiddlesticks. I didn't think he would do that. He's been calling here for the past hour."

"I take it you're not ready to speak to him?"

"You take it right. What did he want, anyway?"

Rachel sighed heavily. "He wants you to meet him and Lord Fanston for breakfast in the Coral Restaurant."

"At least we know where not to go for breakfast, then," Marjorie chuckled.

"Have you not eaten yet? I'm sorry, I slept in."

"No. I didn't sleep well; I don't expect you did either. Shall we go to your buffet place? I'm surprised they're still serving breakfast in the Coral Restaurant at this time."

"It's Sunday, I think they stay open later."

"Did Jeremy say whether they have found Lady Fanston?"

"He didn't mention her, but he sounded normal. Frustrated, he hadn't been able to get hold of you, but otherwise normal, so maybe she's turned up after all."

"I do hope so. I've been worried all night."

Lady Fanston wasn't a friend of Marjorie's, but it was still a concern when someone went missing, Rachel thought. Even more so if her friend was fretting about her son being implicated in some way, although Rachel didn't believe Jeremy capable of robbery or murder.

"I'll get ready and be with you in fifteen minutes."

It was actually forty minutes before Rachel and Marjorie were seated at a table in the busy buffet, surrounded by happy holiday chatter. It was hard to imagine amidst all the excitement as the ship crossed the Bay of Biscay that the night before, an elderly lady had disappeared without a trace. No-one on board except those in the know would guess anything was amiss.

Marjorie was quietly picking at her food. She appeared frail, despite looking immaculate in a long-sleeved purple dress. The light smattering of makeup couldn't disguise her eyes lacking the sparkle Rachel was used to. It hurt Rachel, seeing her friend like this.

"You're going to have to speak to Jeremy at some stage, Marjorie. Better to find out what's going on."

"I know, dear. The trouble is, although I have the controlling interest in the business, in my head, it really belongs to Jeremy. I've kept a lid on things up to now, but if he wants to make poor decisions and squander away the money, I'm of a mind to let him. I'm getting too old to keep reining in my son. It will all be his when I'm gone, anyway. It's not as if I need to take any money out; I'm wealthy in my own right. Ralph left me more than enough to live extravagantly for the rest of my days if I want to.

"What's bothering me most is that I was deluded enough to imagine my son wanted to spend some leisure time with his mother and that he had changed. I was even thinking of signing the business over to him sooner rather than later."

"So, what now?"

Marjorie stabbed a prune with her fork, sad eyes fixed on Rachel. "I have to decide whether to stay loyal to my late husband's life's work and protect it, or let my son have it and live with the consequences of whatever happens."

There wasn't anything Rachel could think of to say, so she reached across the table and squeezed Marjorie's hand, letting her know she cared.

"Jeremy's been looking for you." A sharp voice crashed through the moment. Rachel looked up to see Octavia Snellthorpe's narrowed green eyes glaring down at Marjorie. Her pinched nose screwed up as she waited for a reply.

"And good morning to you, too, Octavia." Marjorie gave an innocent smile. "I hope you slept well."

"Did you hear what I said? Your son's in a right mood now, says you ignored his calls and his invitation to breakfast."

Taking no notice of the question or the accusation that she was the reason for Jeremy's ill temper, Marjorie aimed the next missile with the same innocent tone.

"I'm surprised you're not out enjoying the ship's facilities with your husband on our first full sea day. Perhaps there's someone else you might be hoping to meet."

Octavia stepped back, startled. "I don't know what you mean. As I said, you've put Jeremy in a bad mood. No-one wants to be around a man when he's angry."

Marjorie fixed her penetrating gaze on Octavia, head held high. "And you believe it's me he's angry with rather than anyone else?"

"Like who?"

"Like you, perhaps, or Wilfred Vanmeter. I'm too old for your games, Octavia. And look, the man in question appears to be heading in your direction now."

Rachel spun around, and sure enough, Wilfred was making a beeline for their table, beaming at Octavia.

"Hello, d…" he stopped on recognising Marjorie, fear flashing across his dark green eyes.

"Good morning, Lord Vanmeter, we were just talking about you. Weren't we, Octavia?"

"Erm…"

"Why don't you join us?" Marjorie said, face and tone as sharp as a razor.

"Thank you, Lady Snellthorpe, but I was just on my way to meet my cousin," Wilfred blustered.

"How is Tom? Has Lady Fanston been found?" Rachel intervened before Marjorie said something she might regret.

"I'm afraid not. It wouldn't surprise me if someone didn't knock her off for the diamonds she was wearing last night."

"Oh? You recall the events of last night, then? I thought you were rather the worse for wear," Marjorie's tone was accusatory.

"Sorry about that, Lady Snellthorpe. I do sometimes drink too much, but I remember the events of last night.

Every minute, as a matter of fact," he winked at Octavia, who scowled.

"Did I see you leave the party at one stage? People seemed to be coming and going so much, I wondered if there was something going on elsewhere. Cooking up a surprise for Lady Fanston, perhaps?" It was Rachel's turn to play the innocent. There was a flicker of a twitch in Wilfred's right eye before he replied.

"Nothing like that. I just went for a breath of fresh air, that's all."

"And you didn't see Lady Fanston on your travels?" Rachel pressed.

"Why would I? She was in her room, wasn't she? Or maybe she'd already gone over the side by then. If you'll excuse me, I really must be going." Wilfred made a hasty retreat back the way he'd come.

"He is a most unpleasant man, sober and drunk. Let's hope no foolish woman is taken in by his pretence; he's a nasty piece of work," Marjorie said pointedly.

Octavia ignored the barb, huffed, and stormed off in the opposite direction to Wilfred.

"Silly girl," said Marjorie. "What do you make of the bullish Wilfred Vanmeter?"

"Not a lot, if I'm honest. Same as you: he's a flirt, a drunk and a liar, but that doesn't mean he's involved in Lady Fanston's disappearance."

"The liar part referring to his supposed whereabouts when he left the party, I assume. I just hope my ridiculous daughter-in-law did nothing stupid. Anyway, enough of this talk. Shall we do some investigating, or would you rather leave it to the ship's security?"

"I'm inclined to leave it to Waverley and his team. I thought about it a lot during the night. Lady Fanston may well have fallen or jumped over the side, and even if someone killed her, it's none of our business." Rachel was worried about a conflict of interest with Jeremy and Octavia being on the suspect list if foul play was involved. If she were to investigate, her objectivity would be called into question, and she wouldn't want to do anything to upset Marjorie any more than she had been upset already by Jeremy and Octavia's behaviour.

"On this occasion, I agree with you. I won't speak ill of the dead, but that woman and her husband have caused me nothing but trouble and we've only been away a day. How about a spa day? Jeremy will never find us in there. My treat."

Rachel wasn't sure whether Marjorie's avoidance of her son could go on for too much longer, but she knew her friend. When Marjorie dug her heels in, she was unlikely to budge until she was good and ready. Rachel would be there when she was.

"Why not? Let's go under the radar for the day, it will be fun. I could do with a bit of pampering."

Chapter 11

It was the third full sea day and they would dock in their first port tomorrow. Four days since they'd boarded, but apart from running around the track on deck sixteen each morning, Rachel had barely ventured outside, spending her time with Marjorie in the spa or the theatre, where her friend booked private boxes each evening so they could remain incognito. They had eaten their evening meals in the speciality dining restaurants, paying the surcharge.

With Marjorie still being determined to play hide and seek with Jeremy, they had also avoided bumping into any of the Fanston party. It had initially been challenging for Rachel not to call Waverley, resisting the urge to find out what had become of Lady Fanston, but now she had pushed the entire business to the back of her mind. Her only mission was to reunite Marjorie with her son before the cruise was over. There was still plenty of time for that, but what worried Rachel was that Jeremy had not made any further attempts to contact his mother.

Rachel climbed out of the pool and joined Marjorie for late afternoon tea. Leisure time in the spa had been a welcome break, although she would have enjoyed it more if she didn't have to keep checking in every direction to make sure they weren't found out by any of the people they were avoiding. This couldn't go on.

She approached the subject tentatively. "Marjorie, as much as I've loved the past few days," she began, drying her hair with a towel and dripping water onto the floor, "I think it's time to come out of hiding. We're docking in Alicante tomorrow and I don't want to be looking over my shoulder the whole time we're ashore."

Marjorie sipped her tea, staring into the deep blue pool. "You're quite right, dear. It's time. We'll dine in the main restaurant tonight, and if we don't see Jeremy there, I promise I'll call him before morning. He's clearly not going to call me."

Rachel exhaled, relieved that she hadn't been met with resistance. It had never been her intention to come between mother and son, but she feared the longer this situation went on, the more likely Jeremy would be to hold her responsible. Even if he didn't, Octavia would. She felt her muscles relax, realising just how tense she had been, dreading the inevitable conversation. But just like her father always said, things were never as bad when confronted.

"That's a relief. I'm sure it's for the best."

"I couldn't face another speciality dinner anyway, far too rich for my liking," Marjorie faced her and chuckled. "Besides, my curiosity has got the better of me. I want to know what happened to that Colleen Fanston woman. You would have thought that irritating man would have kept us informed, wouldn't you?"

Rachel laughed. "By that irritating man, I take it you mean Chief Waverley. Why should he? We're not on his team." Rachel remembered the tremor in his hand when she thought of the chief. She wished Sarah were on board so she could ask her about it. "Not to mention the small matter of us playing *safe house*, behaving like we're in witness protection."

"Well, he jolly well should be looking for us. I bet he's still fumbling about in the dark like he always does. After all the times we've helped him, the least he could do is keep us updated."

"Hang on a minute. I thought we didn't want to know about it or get involved. Isn't that partly why we're avoiding all contact with humanity? Coming out of hiding isn't going to change your resolve on that score, I hope."

"Of course not, but I still think he should keep us informed."

"Marjorie Snellthorpe, you're exasperating at times. That poor man can't win."

"And why should he? I know I can be trying, but you wouldn't have me any other way."

Rachel tapped Marjorie's teacup with her mug. "You're right on that score. Here's to you being you and me being me."

Marjorie laughed before taking another sip of tea.

***

Rachel was delighted to see Jeremy and Octavia at their dinner table when they were shown through by the maître d'. This was actually the first time she and Marjorie had been to the Coral Restaurant since boarding. Jeremy stood as a grinning waiter pulled back the two women's chairs.

"Welcome to your table, ladies. My name is Juan and it will be my pleasure to serve you this evening." The friendly waiter made sure they were seated comfortably.

"Glad to see you decided to join us," Jeremy said tentatively, half-smiling, with eyes fixed on his mother.

"We've had a lovely few days sampling the alternative cuisine the ship has to offer," said Marjorie, as if there had never been any argument.

Jeremy nodded. "Hello again, Rachel. I hope my mother hasn't been driving you mad."

"On the contrary, we've been enjoying ourselves... but she did want to see more of the family," she added quickly.

Octavia looked glum. "I'm glad you've been entertaining yourselves; we've done nothing for three whole days. Utterly boring. I'll be pleased to get my feet on firm land tomorrow."

"Sea days can be challenging, particularly if you're an active person," said Rachel, trying to comfort the sullen woman.

"Octavia's not physically active, but we do usually enjoy a good social life," said Jeremy. "We were hoping to see more of Harvey and Tom, but with what's happened to Colleen, they've been keeping themselves to themselves."

Rachel noticed the omission of any mention of Wilfred Vanmeter or his mother.

"And what has happened to Colleen? Did you find out?" Marjorie's inquisitiveness had clearly got the better of her, although Rachel had to admit she was dying to know what had gone on as well.

Jeremy appeared sad. "I don't know, not exactly. When I did manage to see Harvey, he told me they've informed him she's missing, presumed drowned. They're still hoping a body will be washed ashore. When I spoke to the security chappy earlier, he said the tides have changed which makes it more likely she'll be found, presuming she went in the water."

"Where else could she be?" Octavia snapped. "She's hardly gone incognito on board the ship, has she? Poor Colleen."

"I don't suppose so," said Jeremy.

"Well, I, for one, miss her. If she'd been on board, at least I'd have had someone to shop with."

"You really don't need to be doing any more shopping, Octavia. Enough's enough." Jeremy's voice had risen a few decibels. He cleared his throat. "Sorry, darling, I don't mean to shout, but we have to face the fact that Colleen has most probably drowned. Curbing your shopping could be a way of showing respect."

"How awful to go overboard. It was perishingly cold that night. Unfortunate woman," said Marjorie. "What about her sister, Melody? Is she consoling Lord Fanston and Tom?" Marjorie also omitted to mention the elephant in the room: Wilfred Vanmeter.

"I don't know. As I said, Harvey's been distant since it all happened. We met for breakfast the morning after the party, but he was too agitated to eat, or talk for that matter. I haven't really seen him since then, other than to ask if there's been any news. He's been a bit off with us, if I'm honest. Whenever I see Tom, he turns in the opposite direction. Probably doesn't want to be reminded about the dreadful business."

"Will they be leaving the ship when we get into port tomorrow, do you know?" asked Rachel.

Before Jeremy got the chance to answer, the waiters arrived to take drinks and meal orders. Rachel reluctantly turned her attention to the à la carte menu. As usual, there was plenty of choice of starters, main courses and extras if one wanted. A selection of bread appeared on the table while they studied the options. Rachel always preferred to eat in the buffet where it was less formal, but she and Marjorie had avoided it in case they ran into Octavia and Wilfred again.

She was still musing when the waiter reached her.

"Rachel?" Marjorie snapped her away from her thoughts.

"Oh, sorry, I was miles away. Could I have a shrimp cocktail starter, followed by sea bass, please?"

"I'll have the mussels followed by orange-infused teriyaki chicken. That sounds interesting," said Marjorie.

Once they had all placed their orders, Jeremy raised his glass in the air.

"Let's toast the rest of the holiday. Shall we do something together tomorrow?"

"That would be nice," said Marjorie, clearly softening now her son was away from Harvey Fanston's influence. "Perhaps we could hire a car to show us the sights."

"Splendid idea," said Jeremy, as they clinked glasses.

Octavia brightened. "We could also do a bit of shopping."

Jeremy sighed.

"Perhaps," said Marjorie, winking at Rachel. "Did you answer Rachel's question about whether the Fanston party is leaving tomorrow? I'm not sure I heard."

"I think they might be," Jeremy said. "Harvey and Tom at least, I'm not sure about anyone else."

"I can't say I blame them. It hardly turned out to be the big anniversary bash they'd been hoping for, did it?" Marjorie added, "I hope you're not too disappointed, Jeremy."

"If you're referring to the business proposition, not at all. It was probably a madcap idea in the first place, although it would have worked well for us." Jeremy beamed at his mother, but Rachel suspected it was all show; his eyes told her he was bitterly disappointed. "The business is thriving, Mother, and I'm hoping to expand it into Europe."

"Let's not talk about that now," said Marjorie.

Jeremy looked towards his wife as if they had a secret. "No need to, Mother. I'm sure it will all work out."

Rachel wondered what he meant by that. Was he going to push ahead with whatever he and Lord Fanston had been plotting? Marjorie showed no interest in pursuing the conversation, and as Rachel didn't feel it was her place to do so, they spent the rest of their time over dinner making plans for the next day.

After the most peaceful evening she'd had since coming on board, Rachel went to her room happy. At least, she was until a knock sounded at her door and she saw through the spyglass who was on the other side.

Chapter 12

Rachel opened the door of her suite to let a sombre-looking Jack Waverley inside. He didn't need to say anything; his face told her Lady Fanston's body had been found, but why the sympathetic look? He knew Lady Fanston wasn't a close friend of hers, or Marjorie's.

"I'm sorry to bother you at this late hour, Rachel, but I have bad news…" he coughed. "I think you should hear it."

"I take it they've found a body. Is it definitely Lady Fanston?" She followed Waverley into her sitting room. Shoulders hunched, gait slow, his body language screamed deflated. Here was a man carrying the weight of the world on his shoulders, but why?

"A fishing boat pulled the body of an elderly female from the water earlier this afternoon and alerted the coastguard. The coastguard has since returned it to land, and from the description of what the dead woman was wearing, we believe it is Lady Fanston. Do you mind if we sit down?"

They were standing awkwardly in the centre of the lounge. "Of course. Can I get you a drink?"

"I'll have a Scotch, if you don't mind. I think you should have one too."

Rachel raised an eyebrow. This was clearly not a routine visit to tell her about the body. She poured the chief a whisky, but opted for still water for herself. Handing his drink to him, she took the chair opposite and poured her water into a glass.

"There's obviously more to the story than finding Lady Fanston's body. Should I call Marjorie?"

His head shot up, startled, and he raised his voice slightly. "No. At least, not yet. Let me explain."

Rachel waited impatiently while Waverley took a swallow of his whisky. The hand shaking was more pronounced.

"Chief… Jack," she softened her voice, "I've been meaning to ask: is there something wrong with your hand?"

Waverley put the glass down and forced his hand to be still, clutching it with the other. His eyes looked fearful.

"What makes you ask that?"

"I've noticed you seem to have a tremor. Have you seen Dr Bentley about it?"

"Can't say I've noticed anything like that, must be stress."

Rachel held the palm of her hand up. "Look, it's fine if you don't want to talk about it with me, but I think you should see someone. I noticed it in December on the New Year cruise; it's not a new thing you can put down to stress." Rachel watched as Waverley turned his eyes on to the straw-coloured drink in his glass and drained it. She hoped to God it wasn't anything to do with his drinking.

"Point taken. Now can we get back to the matter at hand?"

"Please do," said Rachel, respecting his wish to leave the subject of his health.

"As I said before, we believe Lady Fanston's body has been recovered, but there are some anomalies I need to warn you about."

"Warn me?" she stifled a grin. "That sounds ominous."

"Someone had strangled lady Fanston. Post Mortem will tell us whether she died from strangulation or whether she died from drowning, but—"

"But what?"

"You need to prepare yourself… or rather, you need to prepare Lady Snellthorpe."

"Now you're worrying me." Rachel stared at her water, wishing she had chosen something stronger after all.

"She was strangled with a man's tie, which was still on her person. I'm afraid it was a very specific man's tie: designer, and purple, I'm informed. Photographs have identified it as having been worn by a guest earlier that day."

Rachel's heart sank.

"And the man's name?"

Waverley coughed. "Jeremy Snellthorpe. I'm sorry to say we have arrested Lord Snellthorpe on suspicion of murder."

Rachel opened her mouth to speak, but words wouldn't come out. She went to the fridge and poured herself a brandy, automatically handing Waverley another whisky. All she could think of was how devastated Marjorie would be. Now it was her hands that were trembling. Just when Marjorie and Jeremy had made up following the disagreement earlier in the cruise.

"It can't have been Jeremy."

"Why not?" asked Waverley.

"Because I don't believe he's capable of murder."

"You should know better than anyone, Rachel. The most unlikely people are capable of murder. You meet with it every day in your job. What we don't know yet is whether her death was intentional or the result of a robbery that got out of hand."

"You say he was wearing the tie earlier in the day? Jeremy wore a tuxedo and bow tie that evening. Surely, anyone could have taken his tie and used it to strangle the poor woman? Even another woman." Rachel's thoughts turned to Octavia. Would she be capable of murder? Somehow, she had less difficulty believing Octavia could be responsible than Jeremy. "You mentioned a robbery. I take it they didn't find the diamonds on the body."

"Unfortunately, bodies swell when they've been in salt water for a few days, so we don't know whether the necklace snapped off in the water or whether it was stolen."

Something didn't sound right. "And the earrings?"

"They are also missing. They were clip-ons, so could have come off in a struggle or when she hit the water."

"How come the tie stayed in place if everything else is missing? And why would a killer allow the murder weapon to go into the water with her?"

"The tie had entangled itself around her arm as if she'd tried to pull it away from her neck. As for why it went into the water, who knows? He could have been disturbed, or perhaps he just panicked. Maybe she wasn't meant to die."

"There's a lot of supposition in these theories, Chief."

"I realise that, Rachel, and I'm not completely convinced myself, but it's out of my hands. Lord Snellthorpe will be handed over to the Spanish authorities tomorrow and detectives from the UK are flying in to question him. I don't make the rules. I'm sorry."

"Can I speak to Jeremy before I break any of this to Marjorie?"

Waverley looked doubtful, shaking his head slightly.

"You owe me, Chief. Please, there's not much time if you're handing him over tomorrow."

"All right, Rachel, but I want Inglis present to take notes."

"He might not talk if someone else is there," Rachel protested.

"That's my offer. Take it or leave it."

Waverley stood up, showing the conversation was over.

"Okay, I'll take it. Do you know if the rest of the Fanston party is leaving tomorrow? When I spoke to Jeremy earlier, he was under the impression most of them were."

"Now they know there's nothing more they can do and that we've arrested Jeremy Snellthorpe, they've decided to stay on board as far as Athens. Apparently, Lady Fanston had family there and Lord Fanston wants to break it to them personally. Quite handy, really, we can get detailed statements from Lord Fanston about—" he hesitated.

"It's okay. You don't need to hide anything from me. I'd want to know about Jeremy's state of mind and behaviour leading up to Lady Fanston's suspicious disappearance if I suspected him of murder. Interesting, they've changed their minds about leaving, though."

"Why?"

"It's almost as if, now the heat's off, whoever killed Colleen Fanston can relax. I believe there's a network of diamond fencers in Greece."

"Rachel, I'm warning you, stay out of this. We've got our man whether or not you like it, and if we haven't, let's leave it to the police. Don't go upsetting that family any further. Do you hear me?"

"Yes, Chief." Rachel had no intention of leaving *that* family alone for one minute and couldn't care less about upsetting them. "When can I speak to Jeremy?"

"Go down to the brig in half an hour. I'll let Inglis know to expect you."

At least it's going to be Rosemary Inglis there, she's sensible and knows when to keep her mouth shut, Rachel thought.

***

Rosemary was waiting at the entrance when Rachel arrived downstairs where the brig was situated. The security officer gave her a sympathetic smile.

"Come through to the office and I'll bring him in; there's not much room in the cells."

Rachel stepped inside the office, pleased she didn't have to see Jeremy in a padded cell. She moved a chair away from the desk so it would look less like an interview room and more conducive to conversation.

Jeremy was red-faced and angry when he arrived. "Rachel, how did you get down here? Never mind. I have no idea what's going on around here or how that idiot of a security chief can think I killed anyone."

Rosemary stood against the door, blocking any attempt by Jeremy to escape if he had a mind to.

"They found a purple tie belonging to you on Lady Fanston's person, Jeremy. There's evidence someone strangled her."

"So they said, but it wasn't me. I had no reason to strangle the woman. I can't believe anyone would think for one minute I would do such a thing." Jeremy was behaving bullishly. She would get nowhere with him in this mood.

"Why don't you sit down and talk to me, then I'll see what I can do."

Jeremy clearly debated whether to walk out again. His eyes darted to the broad Rosemary Inglis, arms folded as she blocked the exit, and then back to Rachel.

"I'm sorry. It's not every day one gets accused of murder." He flopped down into a chair, putting his head in his hands. "I can't believe this is happening to me, that's all."

"Start from the beginning. How do you think your tie was used – if indeed it's established that it was used – to strangle Lady Fanston?"

"I've already told them," he glared at Rosemary. "Harvey and Colleen invited us for drinks in their suite when we met them soon after boarding—"

"By us, you mean you and Octavia. Was anyone else there?"

"All of them. It was a cocktail party. Tom and Annette were there, Melody and that prat who's been trying it on with my wife."

"Wilfred Vanmeter?"

Jeremy nodded, lifting his head, and making eye contact for the first time since he had entered.

"It was hot in there – they had turned the heating up; people were drinking a lot. Pratface was smoking on the balcony even though it's not allowed. At some stage, I used the bathroom and took the tie off. I must have hung it over the towel rail or something; it wasn't in my pocket when I got back to my room. I was going to ask about it the next day but with all that had happened, I forgot all about it."

Rachel looked over at Rosemary, who shook her head.

"Okay. So you think you left the tie in the Royal Suite. Surely Octavia can corroborate that?"

"She told the chief she can't remember. Can you believe it? My own wife can't remember what I was wearing."

"I guess the drinks were flowing," suggested Rachel.

"You're right about that. My wife tends to drink too much, especially when trying to impress, and that Vanmeter idiot was plying her with alcohol, hogging her attention," Jeremy spat the words out. "I told her to lay off, but she basically told me to beat it."

Rachel was surprised Wilfred and Octavia had been so obvious in Jeremy's presence, but didn't really have time to delve into the ins and outs of his marriage.

"So, no-one remembers you removing your tie?" Rachel looked hopefully towards Rosemary, who shook her head again.

Jeremy covered his head with his hands once more before rubbing his forehead aggressively. He looked up at Rachel.

"I need a good lawyer, don't I?"

"So far, the evidence is circumstantial. Did you have any reason to kill Lady Fanston?"

Jeremy shook his head vigorously. "No. Why would I? Harvey was going to sell the necklace and invest money in the business."

"Is that what you wanted to discuss with your mother? I think you'd better take a step back and explain why you needed Lord Fanston to invest in the business, and how he could sell a necklace that didn't belong to him."

"I don't know what you mean. According to Harvey, the jewels belonged to him. Colleen was happy to go along with it; she didn't want to keep the diamonds. Too damn tempting for criminals, that's what she said."

More likely Lord Fanston wasn't going to give the gems to his wife, thought Rachel, but didn't break this news yet. Either Jeremy was lying, and he knew that the Fanstons didn't own the diamonds, or the Fanstons had been about to take him to the cleaners.

"You still haven't said why you needed their investment. Marjorie tells me the business is thriving."

Jeremy sighed. "The business is thriving, but all the money's tied up while I'm in a truckload of debt. Please promise you won't tell Mother about this." He wrung his hands, not able to look at her.

"I, erm—"

"Octavia's got expensive tastes. I'm sure Mother's told you that already, but the truth is, she's bled me dry and I can't call in any more loans without putting up the business as surety. If I do that, Mother will find out, and then she'll feel the need to bail me out. I'd be too ashamed to face her." He wiped a tear away from his eye. "That business is my father's life's work – I'm sure you've heard that before too," bitterness crept into his voice. "I don't want to lose it to pay for any more of my wife's extravagances, but the creditors are knocking at my door and I have no way of paying them."

"So, a cash investment from someone like the Fanstons would be the answer to all your prayers?" Rachel suggested.

"Exactly. If I let Harvey get on the board of directors, he'll put five hundred thousand pounds into the business and give me a two hundred thousand golden handshake, enough to pay off all my debts and leave some over. So you see, I had no reason to kill Colleen. Harvey was my lifeline."

Rachel didn't have the heart to tell him that this news strengthened the case against him, rather than weakening it, providing a powerful motive for murder, especially if the diamonds didn't belong to Lord and Lady Fanston in the first place.

"Have you discussed your debt with your wife?"

"I've tried, but she doesn't listen. She knows the business is worth a fortune and that I stand to inherit Mother's wealth, so she just thinks she can go on spending money like it comes out of a tap. You heard her over dinner: it's shopping this and shopping that. She's already built up a huge on-board credit-card bill. I can't get her to listen, and now she's besotted with that Vanmeter fellow who reinforces her view that everything comes easily when you're rich. But I'm not rich. At least, not yet. And believe it or not, I want my mother to live forever."

"Okay, so let's assume you didn't do it. Who do you think would have wanted the necklace badly enough to strangle Lady Fanston and throw her off the ship?"

"My money would be on that Wilfred Vanmeter. He's a leech if ever I met one. Lives off his mother, has extravagant tastes in women, cars and holidays, but doesn't have a job."

"Is Melody Vanmeter wealthy?"

"I wouldn't know, it's not the sort of thing one asks. She must be, if she's Colleen's sister. Their family has a tonne of money. Rachel, whatever you do, please don't tell Mother about the debt, and don't tell her they have arrested me until I've been moved in the morning."

"Are you sure Colleen Fanston had money of her own?"

"Not sure, no, but I've always assumed so. She gave that impression."

"What's Octavia going to do now?"

"I suggested she fly home tomorrow and get hold of a good criminal lawyer."

"I'll try to keep the debt from Marjorie, but I can't lie to her, Jeremy, she'd never forgive me."

"Just do what you can." He stood up, indicating to Rosemary he wanted to go back to the brig.

"Just one more question. Why did you say you went to the gents when you went missing for a while?"

Jeremy sighed. "Because I didn't want to go into detail. Truth is, I needed some air. I'd told Harvey Mother might take some persuading to let him in on the business and he didn't like that, so he had stormed off. Then I turned around and saw my wife giggling with Vanmeter. It was either go over and thump him, or get out and cool off. I decided on the latter. When Mother asked where I'd gone, I didn't want to admit I went off in a huff." Jeremy's head dropped as he walked towards the door. Turning back, he said, "Rachel, Mother tells me you're good at your job. Please find out who did this. And keep Mother safe, will you?"

"That I can promise," said Rachel.

Chapter 13

Sleep eluded Rachel; she tossed and turned all night with multiple theories and scenarios going through her head. If Jeremy was telling the truth – and she believed he was – then someone else had most likely stolen the diamond necklace and earrings. The murderer was doing a good job of setting Jeremy up as the fall guy; whether this was by design or opportunity after he had left his tie in the bathroom, would still need to be established. If the gems hadn't been stolen, there had to be another motive for killing Lady Fanston.

Rachel's chief concern was how Marjorie would react to the news of her son's arrest and whether it would drive an even bigger wedge between her friend and the security chief. She wished she could just disembark in Alicante and take Marjorie home, but that would leave the killer aboard ship and in an excellent position to sell the diamonds on. Jeremy had asked her to find the perpetrator, and she had to do just that; not only for his sake, but for his mother's, her dear friend.

Following an early morning run around deck sixteen, Rachel wandered into the onboard gym.

"Rachel! I didn't know you were on board." Brad, the Australian fitness instructor she'd met on the previous cruise, pulled her into a warm embrace. He then took her hand and led her along the corridor to the staffroom. "Look who's here, guys."

Ethan leapt out of his chair, almost knocking over a drink on the table, and hugged her tight. "It's so good to see you, Rachel."

She had avoided the gym thus far on the voyage because she had got to know the staff there under false pretences while working undercover. She had been concerned about how they would respond to her as she had deceived them, but it seemed they were still happy to see her. The only person who clearly wasn't pleased to see her was Cassandra Knight. Barely out of her teens, she looked as though she should be in school, and still had a habit of acting like the playground bully, too.

"Look what the cat dragged in," she sneered, glaring at Rachel.

"Oh, grow up," said Rachel once Ethan released her.

"I've got work to do," the young woman retorted before storming from the room.

"She really hates you, doesn't she?" Ethan laughed. "Still hasn't managed to tie this guy down either."

"And she never will. She's too young and childish; I like mature women," said Brad.

"Are you here for a gym session or a catchup?" asked Ethan.

"A catchup and a favour, actually."

"Well, we owe you big time, so we'll help in whatever way we can."

"Have any of these people been in here for fitness sessions or used the gym?" Rachel handed over the list of passengers.

"Annette Elrod, she's definitely been in. I've been working with her on an exercise programme," Brad said. "I've got to know her quite well, as a matter of fact."

"Ooh, you don't say," teased Ethan.

"Not like that, you wuss. She's not my type, but the poor woman's unhappy. I've been a sounding board. Apparently, she's stuck in a regrettable marriage. Her husband plays away with other women, but they keep up a charade of being a happy couple to convince his grandma they're the perfect match. Once the grandma's snuffed it, he's promised her a good settlement and they'll get divorced. Apparently, the grandma doesn't believe in divorce."

Rachel scrunched up her face. "From what I've heard, the grandma *is* divorced."

Brad frowned. "I'm pretty sure that's what she said."

"How come she told you all that?" Rachel asked.

"Gym instructors are like therapists. Clients can tell us what they like and it goes no further. At least, not to anyone they care about. I don't recognise any of the other names on that list, except the guy with the surname Elrod. I'm guessing that's Annette's husband, but he's not been in here."

"This guy's been in here a lot." Ethan tapped the list next to Wilfred Vanmeter's name. "With her: Octavia Snellthorpe. I think they're having a fling; they're certainly not here for the exercise. Every time I see them, they're giggling and touchy-feely, if you know what I mean?"

"I'm afraid I know exactly what you mean," Rachel replied. "Her husband told me she doesn't like physical exercise."

"Maybe not the type he's thinking of, at least," laughed Ethan.

"Keep it clean, Ethan," Rachel scolded. "What about any of the others?"

"Nope, don't recognise their names. Is there anything we can do to help?"

"Not really, unless you see one of them trying to pawn some diamonds," she chuckled. "I don't suppose you've had any diamond smugglers telling you their secrets?"

"Ha, ha. Are you working undercover again?" Ethan quizzed.

"Not as such, no. I'm on holiday, but a crime has been committed."

"And that's your suspect list?" Brad suggested.

"Sort of. Anyway, it was good to see you guys, and thanks for the information. I'll drop in again for some exercise."

"You're looking pretty good to me," said Ethan, leaning in for another hug.

"Knock it off, Ethan. You know she's happily married," Brad scolded.

Ethan grinned. "Can't blame a guy for trying."

"As you can see, Rachel, some things haven't changed. We'll keep our ears to the ground if they come in again, and let you know if we hear anything."

"Thanks, I'd appreciate it, but I think Octavia Snellthorpe's getting off today."

"I don't think so. Her boyfriend was in here half an hour ago, booking them in for the studio later. Well after we set sail," Ethan said. "He's a bit of an exercise freak, but whether he's just trying to impress the lady, I can't work out. For a skinny fella, he can lift some serious weights. When they're in together, though, they book the studio."

Rachel felt her temper rising, partly for Marjorie's sake, but mostly this time for Jeremy. Octavia had fleeced him dry, and was now seemingly happy to leave him taking the blame for a crime he didn't commit while she carried on a silly affair with Wilfred Vanmeter.

"In that case, if you do hear anything of interest going on between those two, I'd appreciate a heads up. I'm not interested in their relationship, though, unless they mention framing her husband."

"Ooh, nasty. I'll be sure to listen in and let you know if that topic crops up. I wouldn't hold out much hope, though. All I've heard so far is sweetie this, darling that and ooh, look at those muscles."

Rachel scowled. "I think I'm going to be sick." She left the gym feeling furious, and not sure how helpful the information was. Ethan had merely confirmed her suspicions that Wilfred and Octavia were having an affair, but she couldn't see either of them being clever enough to fence diamonds. For that, one needed contacts. Still, both were apparently callous enough to carry on seeing each other while Jeremy was being accused of murder.

The information about Tom and Annette's marriage was more interesting and probably more useful, but not new, as Marjorie had already discovered most of that. How would Tom feel if his grandmother had given the diamonds to her son or daughter-in-law rather than leaving them to him? Was Grandma Elrod playing them along for some mischievous reason as yet unknown? She would need to delve into Tom's grandmother as one part of her inquiry, and she knew just the man for the job.

***

The moment Rachel had been dreading finally came when she joined Marjorie for breakfast in her suite. Marjorie was full of joy, so excited at the prospect of spending the day with her son. Rachel's heart pounded, breaking with sorrow for her friend.

"It's a pity Octavia will be joining us for the day, but I suppose we must bear these trials. She'll want to go shopping, of course, and spend more of Jeremy's money."

Rachel grimaced, remembering Jeremy's revelations about his debt and Octavia's spending habits. She checked her watch impatiently, willing the time away.

Here goes, she thought, assuming that by now he would be in the hands of the Alicante authorities.

"Marjorie, I have something to tell you. You're not going to like it."

Marjorie looked up from pouring a third cup of tea.

"They've cancelled," she sighed. "I might have known it was too good to be true."

"Not exactly. Lady Fanston's body was discovered yesterday and I'm afraid there's no easy way to tell you this, but Jeremy's been arrested." Rachel checked Marjorie's face for a reaction. Despite a slight pursing of the lips, she remained in control, and Rachel could only admire her friend.

"You'd better start from the beginning."

"After I got back to my room last night, Waverley paid me a visit." Rachel told her what Waverley had said about Lady Fanston's body being found by fishermen, its removal to land, and finally about the suspected cause of death and Jeremy's tie being the probable murder weapon. "So you see, the chief felt he had no choice but to arrest him."

Marjorie snorted. "No choice indeed! There will be some innocent explanation. I need to speak to Jeremy."

Rachel took Marjorie's now trembling hand. "He'll be ashore by now. British detectives are going to question him sometime today."

"Will they deport him? Do you think we should leave? I'll need to speak to a lawyer. I really don't believe Jeremy is capable of murder, and even if he were, he wouldn't be stupid enough to strangle the woman with his own tie and let it go over the side with the body."

Rachel wasn't sure which question to answer, so she took a deep breath, praying she would be able to say the right thing and comfort her. "Waverley let me visit Jeremy last night, and you're right. Jeremy says he took the tie off after joining the Fanstons for drinks in their suite on boarding day; that's when he and Octavia got the invite for dinner. He believes he left it in the bathroom."

"So my son did not use the murder weapon. Even the bumbling Chief Waverley should have established that, surely?"

Rachel shook her head, frowning. "Unfortunately, no-one recalls Jeremy removing the tie and they all deny seeing it after the drinks party. Even Octavia couldn't remember."

"Too drunk, I suppose, all of them. Was it just the Fanstons?"

"No. They were all there, and Waverley questioned every one of them, hoping someone would confirm Jeremy's account; he really didn't want to arrest your son."

"Humph. Well, that's something, but I still think he's jumped the gun, just like he always does. So, what's his theory of motive: that Jeremy killed her for the jewels?"

Rachel nodded. "The necklace and earrings weren't on the body, but it's unclear whether the necklace snapped and went in the water or was stolen. The same could have happened to the earrings as they were clip-ons, but I can't see it being anything other than robbery. Perhaps one that went wrong."

"Unless the plan was to kill Colleen Fanston all along and make it look like a robbery. Perhaps the killer wasn't interested in the diamonds at all." Marjorie's eyes pleaded with Rachel. "There must be something we can do."

"Jeremy asked me not to tell you until he was ashore; he didn't want you to see him in the ship's brig. He asked me to investigate, and I will, but if you want to go and be with him, I will understand."

Rachel could see the conflict raging through Marjorie's mind as she stood and paced the room for a few minutes. Eventually, she turned.

"We will be of more use to him staying and finding out who did this. Why frame Jeremy? That's what I don't understand."

"I've been wondering about that myself. It probably wasn't part of the plan, but the tie in the bathroom provided the killer with a murder weapon and a scapegoat."

"The obvious thing would be to look for the diamonds. I assume they did not find them in Jeremy's room?"

"No."

"So why arrest him?"

Rachel replied gently, "Because his tie was most likely used to strangle the woman. Motive is assumed, not proven."

"Well then, we need to find out the motive. If it's the theft of the diamonds, it could be any one of those greedy pretenders. But what if it's more personal? If that were the case, it would have to be Harvey Fanston. You said he was agitated when he came back to the party after his flit?"

"He was, but I think he and Jeremy had argued before leaving separately, so it could have been something to do with the business plan. If only we knew what time Lady Fanston was killed, it would help us narrow it down. Waverley must have statements as to where each of them says they were when they left the room. I suppose Harvey Fanston could have tired of his wife, but they seemed happy enough."

"Mm, looks can be deceiving," said Marjorie. "Did Jeremy tell you what he and Harvey Fanston argued about?"

"Not really," Rachel didn't want to mention the part involving Marjorie needing persuading, it would sound unkind. "We didn't get into that much detail. He was obviously upset at being arrested."

"And angry, I suppose. What was the business proposition?"

Rachel had wrestled with how to tell Marjorie about this without breaking her promise to Jeremy.

"Lord Fanston wanted to invest half a million pounds into the business. He was going to put in the money as a cash injection. Jeremy had plans to expand into Europe." Rachel didn't mention the personal handout Jeremy would have received had the deal gone through.

"I see, and what did he want in return?"

"A place on the board."

"Okay, that all makes sense, but where was the money coming from? I still don't believe Harvey Fanston has any money of his own, and from what we've heard from Tom, he's unlikely to be on the receiving end, even after his mother dies."

"The Fanstons were going to sell the diamonds."

Marjorie sat down again and sipped tea. "But they didn't belong to them."

"That's the part we can't be sure about. We need to find out. Why was she wearing them if they weren't hers? Did she steal or borrow them from her mother-in-law, or did Grandma Elrod renege on her deal with Tom? We only have Wilfred and Tom's word that everything was going to Tom. We don't even know how much money's involved. The diamonds could be a minor part of Grandma Elrod's fortune, in which case, she might easily have given them to her son—"

"Tom told me his parents visited his grandmother the day before the cruise," Marjorie said.

"I suggest it's time for us to do our due diligence and find out what was really going on beneath the surface on the night of the party. I detected undercurrents that are beginning to make more sense now. We need to narrow our suspect list down, and the only way to do that is to start digging."

"There's only one problem with that," said Marjorie. "I'm going to be *persona non grata* with Harvey Fanston and Tom if they are innocent and believe my son killed Lady Fanston."

"I've considered that, and we'll need to test the waters there, but you can still speak to Wilfred Vanmeter. He didn't seem to care much about Lady Fanston's death. I don't know how close his mother was to her sister, so we'll need to play that one by ear. I'm sure you could speak to Annette and Octavia.

"I gleaned some interesting information about Annette and Tom's marriage from my friends in the gym. It seems Wilfred's insinuation that their union isn't a happy one is right, and also the bit about Tom being unfaithful. The interesting part – and I think Tom might have implied this to you – is that they have an agreement in place regarding his upcoming inheritance. They pretend to be happily married until Grandma Elrod passes, and then Annette gets a good part of the fortune when they divorce." Rachel explained all that Brad had told her, avoiding any mention of Octavia and Wilfred and their affair, although she knew it was only a matter of time before her astute friend would have her suspicions confirmed.

"Is Octavia leaving today?" Marjorie quizzed.

"Apparently not." Rachel was pleased Marjorie didn't ask how she knew, or she would have had to have mentioned the gym excursions, but annoyed with Octavia for putting her in this position. She hated keeping things from her dear friend, but there was only so much bad news a person could take in one day.

"In which case, I imagine we're still going out with the dratted woman."

"Good thinking, Marjorie. We can start with her," said Rachel, pleased to have something to be getting on with.

Chapter 14

Octavia, dressed for the warmer weather in navy cropped trousers and a loose flowing short-sleeved hot-pink shirt, was already waiting for them by guest services. Her hair was neatly arranged to show off substantial sapphire earrings. Hardly looking like a woman whose husband had been arrested on suspicion of murder fewer than twelve hours ago, she had taken the time to apply plenty of makeup, and a bright red lipstick was making her already full lips stick out like those of a film star.

"There you are, Mother. I thought you'd never arrive." Octavia leaned down to post two air-kisses above each of Marjorie's cheeks.

Rachel felt Marjorie bristle. "Good morning, Octavia. We weren't sure you would be able to make it under the circumstances."

Octavia ignored Rachel's presence, which amused her and gave her an excellent opportunity to watch on.

"Oh, that's nothing. I'm sure it's all a misunderstanding; the lawyers will sort it out. There's no use sitting in my room crying, is there? We have to grin and bear it for now."

"Something you seem to be finding remarkably easy," muttered Marjorie, while Octavia turned her attention to the brochure in her hand. In a louder voice, Marjorie said, "I had wondered if you might travel home today?"

Octavia's incredulous look spoke volumes. "Why would I do that? We've paid for a luxury cruise! One of us might as well enjoy it."

Unbelievable, thought Rachel. The stupid woman didn't even have the decency to try to pretend to her mother-in-law that she was at least partially upset about her husband being locked away somewhere. If Octavia hadn't been a person of interest on her suspect list, she'd have been tempted to tell her exactly what she thought of her and get her out of Marjorie's sight. As things stood, though, perhaps her inappropriate contempt would turn out to be useful. Rachel hoped so.

"Shall we go, then?" Marjorie suggested.

Octavia hesitated, flicking through the brochure again. "Erm… I thought I could go paragliding this morning, and then there's a wine tasting and tapas tour this afternoon. Take a look." She pushed the opened brochure into Marjorie's hands. Marjorie browsed the afternoon trip she was referring to while Octavia continued to behave as if Rachel wasn't there.

Marjorie handed back the brochure. "I'm a little too old for paragliding, my dear, but I'm sure Rachel could accompany you."

Finally, having to acknowledge Rachel's presence, Octavia looked at her with disdain. "No need. Wilfred said he'll take me. How about we meet up at the Plaza Portal de Elche at noon for the wine and tapas?"

"I was under the impression we were going to hire a car for the day and tour the sights," said Marjorie.

Pouting her lips, Octavia played her trump card, becoming the upset wife for the first time. "We were, but when my husband was arrested last night, I was so upset, Wilfred offered to cheer me up. He said the paragliding is amazing and thought it would help take my mind off things."

I bet he did, thought Rachel, saying, "Come on, Marjorie, we can take a tour ourselves. We'll meet you at twelve," she gave Octavia a scathing look.

"Can you believe her behaviour?" Marjorie complained as Rachel led her away. "Paragliding, indeed! How dare she? I hope the blasted parachute thing has a hole in it. I suppose this means she's having an affair with Wilfred Vanmeter, or soon will be."

"You told me she was bad, but I never imagined she would be quite like this," said Rachel. "I got the impression she and Jeremy were well suited with their extravagant tastes and interests."

"To be honest, I thought so too. This cruise has been an eye-opener in so many ways. No wonder Jeremy spends so much money. The woman's a bottomless pit! Oh look, there's Captain Jenson."

Rachel turned to see the captain heading their way.

"Good morning, ladies. I'm so sorry about what has happened to your son, Lady Snellthorpe. Would you mind joining me for coffee?"

"We were just about to go ashore, but that's very kind of you," said Marjorie.

"It won't take long. I have news."

Captain Jenson's insistence was intriguing. Rachel and Marjorie accepted the offer and followed him past guest services to a private room behind the purser's office. Tea and coffee were laid out on a tray. Waverley was talking to someone, and when the other man turned around to greet them, Marjorie rushed over to hug him.

"Jeremy! I thought you were in a Spanish jail or on your way back to England," she exclaimed, standing awkwardly in her son's stiff embrace.

"I would have been if it wasn't for these two gentlemen and an astute security officer."

"Why don't we take a seat and I'll explain?" suggested Captain Jenson. They all did so while a waiter, who had been standing in the background, poured their drinks, then left.

"I only heard this morning you'd been arrested, and now you're here. Free, I hope," Marjorie glared in the direction of Waverley, who nodded.

"Yes, Mother. Hear the captain out."

"Early this morning," Captain Jenson began, "Officer Inglis was studying the guest statements from the night of the dinner party, and those taken yesterday after Lord Snellthorpe told us he'd left his tie in the Royal Suite. She realised no-one had asked the butler whether she had seen the tie."

Marjorie was too pleased and enthralled to shoot Waverley another disparaging look. No doubt he would get an earful about this oversight at a later date.

"The butler, Glenis Komorova, had indeed noticed the tie in the bathroom after the Fanstons left for their evening meal. It wasn't over the towel rail where Lord Snellthorpe had thought it was; it had fallen to the floor and was mixed in among the used towels she was collecting for the laundry. She took the tie through to the lounge and placed it over the back of a chair, believing it belonged to Lord Fanston. She described it accurately to Inglis with no prompting."

"So anyone could have used the tie, which had been placed in full view, to strangle Lady Fanston," said Rachel.

"We have to surmise it was Lord Fanston himself or Thomas Elrod," said the captain. "Working either alone or in cahoots. They are the only two who we know went into the apartment that night."

"What we don't know is the why," explained Waverley. "Which is why we've asked Lord Snellthorpe here to stay out of sight. Captain Jenson has kindly put him up in his guest quarters."

"Which are a lot more comfortable than the brig," laughed Jeremy. "I'm not off the hook completely, but if the chief here can find out who committed the crime, my name will be cleared."

"You want Jeremy to stay out of the way so the murderer thinks they've got away with the crime?" Rachel suggested.

"Exactly that," said the captain. "I can't say I like the idea of them wandering around my ship, but until we have proof of guilt, there's nothing we can do. I can only apologise for the wrongful arrest of your son, Lady Snellthorpe. We felt it important for you to know he is free, but would ask if you could kindly keep the information between yourself and Mrs Jacobi-Prince for the time being. Just while the chief investigates."

"Of course, as long as Jeremy is happy with that. What about Octavia?"

"Erm… it's best if she doesn't know for now," said Captain Jenson. "At your son's request."

"What about the butler, Glenis?" asked Rachel.

"I have instructed her not to say anything and she doesn't know the full story, anyway. Butlers are very good at keeping secrets: they see and hear all manner of things without repeating them."

"Perhaps Rachel and I can help the chief investigate."

Rachel kicked Marjorie gently. "I think we should let the security team do their job, Marjorie."

"Yes, Mother. I don't want you involving yourself in any of this. You go out and enjoy yourself. I'm quite happy with my accommodation, plus it's all on the house." Jeremy smiled, but his face looked drawn. The ordeal of the past twelve hours added to his concerns about debt must be weighing him down.

"If you insist," Marjorie said, stiffly.

"I do."

"And so do I," added Waverley.

"In that case, we'll leave the very able security team to their work. Come on, Rachel, we have some touring to do." Turning to Jeremy, she said, "I'm so pleased to see you. Let's hope the chief brings the matter to a swift conclusion so we can enjoy the rest of our holiday."

"I'd like that, Mother," said Jeremy, his face softening.

***

Rachel left Marjorie and Jeremy alone for a few minutes and took the opportunity to make a telephone call to Carlos while she had a signal. After a quick catchup and an explanation of what had occurred so far, she asked him if he could get some information about Grandma Elrod, her wealth, and whether she had given or loaned the diamond jewellery to Lady Fanston.

"Why can't you just take a holiday like ordinary people without someone turning up dead?" he quizzed, although his tone was good humoured. "Can you tell me anything more about this Grandma Elrod?"

"I'm afraid not, except that she was a Fanston until she divorced some years ago. On that basis, she's Lord Harvey

Fanston's mother and Thomas Elrod, previously Fanston's grandmother. Her husband has since died. Marjorie says she lives in Lincolnshire, not far away from Thomas Elrod, but I can't say where for sure and I daren't ask Waverley for Tom's address."

"He doesn't want you involved, then?"

"Something like that. You know how he blows hot and cold. I think he's worried about Marjorie; she's had such a shock with Jeremy being arrested and now released. I'm not an expert, but I'm assuming Grandma Elrod has a title somewhere. I think Marjorie said Harvey was a baron, whatever that means."

"Don't worry, the aristocracy is easy to trace. I'll start with *Burke's Peerage* and the internet. If they don't turn up there, I'll find someone who works for Lord Fanston. I expect Thomas Elrod's address is in a public record somewhere, so I can track that down and follow that angle as well."

"Thank you, Carlos. I love you."

"I love you too, darling. Stay safe."

"I will. We'll be in Messina in three days' time, so call me then, but if it's urgent, you can contact me via the ship's reception."

"Okay, I'll be happy to put down the paintbrushes for a bit and get on with some investigating. Ciao."

"Bye, Carlos."

Rachel ended the call with a heavy heart. She missed her husband. Looking up to see Marjorie waiting for her, she forced a smile.

"Was that your beloved Carlos you were speaking to?"

"Yep."

"Is he going to help?"

"Yep."

"I take it we're not leaving things to the security team, then?"

"Nope."

"These one-word replies don't suit you, Rachel. Tell me what you're planning."

"First, we go ashore. We've only got an hour now before our meeting with Octavia. Then we work out how to speak to the rest of the people who were there on Saturday evening. I'm not quite so quick as Captain Jenson or Waverley to rule out the rest of them. Any one of them could have arranged to meet Lady Fanston under some pretext or another before stealing the diamonds, strangling her, and putting her over the side. Remember, they all left the room at some point after she did."

"Including my daughter-in-law."

"I'm afraid so, Marjorie. Not that I think she's involved."

"Either way, I fear that marriage is over."

"Yep... Sorry, yes, I think you might be right on that score. Her loss, I suspect."

"And Jeremy's gain. I just hope he sees it that way."

Rachel took Marjorie's arm. "I think he will, if not now, then later. Carlos is going to see what he can discover about Grandma Elrod and the diamonds. In the meantime, come on, Snellthorpe, it's time to do some detective work."

Marjorie patted Rachel's hand appreciatively. "Okay, Holmes, what are we waiting for?"

Chapter 15

Octavia arrived fifteen minutes late, face glowing and eyes bright. Clearly still high, she giggled, "Sorry I'm late. The paragliding session went on longer than expected. It was fabulous. What an experience! I can't wait to tell Jeremy all about it once he's released."

"I should think there are more important matters to be discussed when my son is released," Marjorie scolded.

"What? The business deal? Is it back on, then?"

The gall of the woman would be impressive if it wasn't antagonising Rachel's dear friend.

"I know nothing about *the* deal," retorted Marjorie. "However, I know that my son is going through an *ordeal*, which might make your current behaviour seem thoughtless."

"Jeremy would want me to have a good time; he wouldn't want me moping around."

"And you certainly couldn't be accused of the latter," replied Marjorie.

Rachel could see they were going to lock horns if she wasn't careful. She was at least pleased Octavia believed Jeremy to be innocent, unless she was auditioning for an Oscar-winning performance.

"What's Wilfred doing this afternoon?"

Octavia examined her nails. "Oh, he's gone to meet his mother and the Elrods. They're going to visit some caves or something, I can't remember. If it had been shopping, I would have been tempted to join them. Shall we go shopping instead of the wine and tapas tour?"

"No, we shall not," Marjorie snapped. "Look, there's the guide. I took the liberty of purchasing three tickets before leaving the ship." As Marjorie led Octavia towards a queue of people approaching a woman holding up a sign, she thrust her purse towards Rachel and whispered, "The ticket office is over there. Would you be so kind? I'll keep her under control."

Rachel smirked. "You wily old thing."

"Less of the old."

In a louder voice, Rachel excused herself. "I must find a ladies, I'll catch up with you."

"Okay, dear," Marjorie called.

Octavia barely noticed, still sulking over not going shopping, no doubt. Rachel headed to the ticket office and waited for a couple of family groups to be served before she was able to purchase three tickets. She didn't buy them with Marjorie's money. Her friend was too generous at times and she wouldn't take advantage.

"Enjoy your tour," the amicable woman behind the kiosk said.

"Thanks, I'm looking forward to it."

Rachel sneaked up on Marjorie, who was near the front of the queue, slipping the purse back into her hand.

"I was just saying to Octavia, I gave the tickets to you for safekeeping, Rachel. Do you still have them?"

Rachel waved them in the air just as they reached the guide. The woman checked them before gesturing with her hand towards a man standing close by.

"Welcome to our tour. Your guide is Pedro over there. He will take you around our fabulous bars. Have a brilliant afternoon."

Pedro, a round, cheery-faced man wearing a tour-logoed bright-orange t-shirt, was already carrying a placard with Rachel's surname on it. Thankfully, Octavia didn't notice. He beckoned them over and the three women obliged, joining him on the edge of the square.

"Good afternoon, ladies, my name is Pedro; it is my pleasure to be your guide for the next few hours. Before we begin, you get twenty minutes to enjoy the plaza. It's a beautiful square, no?"

"It is." Rachel loved it already. In the centre stood a round kiosk with a blue-lit canopy covering a circular bar. Tables and chairs were scattered around the square under the canopy of lush-green tropical trees.

"I'll be happy to share the history of the plaza with you if you wish, or you can enjoy it for yourselves."

"Oh, no history, please," said Octavia, yawning. "Are there any shops?"

"Ignore her, Pedro, she's just teasing. I'm Marjorie, this is Rachel and that's my daughter-in-law, Octavia. We'll just wander around for now, if that's all right with you?"

"It's a pleasure to meet you all. Of course it is fine for you to explore on your own." He gave Octavia a tentative glance. "I'll come and find you after twenty minutes, then we will take my air-conditioned vehicle to the next venue where you can have tapas, wine or sangria, all included in the ticket's cost."

"Can't we go now?" Rachel heard Octavia murmuring as Marjorie ushered her into the square, carefully steering the reluctant woman away from Pedro lest she cause offence. This was going to be a long afternoon, but Rachel was sure that once Octavia sampled the local sangria or wines, there would be ample opportunity to pump her for information. Something had to make up for her missing out on a history lesson.

It turned out Pedro was a mine of information, and she and Marjorie enjoyed listening to him wax lyrical about many of the buildings they passed on the journey to the next venue. Octavia, of course, showed no interest in any of the details he imparted as he drove. Once they arrived at the various destinations, Pedro gave them the opportunity inside each bar to have a drink and sample the food.

Rachel was right about Octavia. By the time they stopped at the third bar, Octavia was on her fourth sangria. She declined the wine tasting, which she said was boring, that word seemingly an integral part of her vocabulary. Marjorie and Rachel had been careful at each stop to sample the wine, learn something about its production, bottling, and distribution, and leave their glasses almost full when they left. Octavia was far too self-absorbed to notice. They also made sure they sampled different tapas at each stop, whereas Octavia neglected to eat altogether.

"Silly woman's always on a diet," whispered Marjorie to Rachel. Then they began probing Octavia for information as the woman's tongue loosened.

"Did Wilfred ever find out if Grandma Elrod had given the diamonds to Lady Fanston?" Marjorie asked.

"He doesn't think she would have done. Apparently, the old witch can't stand the woman."

"Couldn't stand the woman," said Marjorie.

"What?"

"Couldn't stand, past tense, dear. Lady Fanston's dead."

"Don't we know it? Almost ruined my cruise, although I do miss her. She was a good friend. She would have gone shopping, you know." Octavia's speech was slurred.

"How well did you know her?" Rachel asked, ignoring the 'good friend' bit which was most likely an exaggeration judging by how fickle Jeremy's wife was. Octavia had become a little more friendly towards her, especially when Rachel bought her an extra sangria that wasn't part of the tour.

"Very well. We shopped together; mixed in the same social groups while Jeremy and Harvey talked business all the time."

"And do you know why Harvey Fanston is interested in Jeremy's business?" Rachel noticed Marjorie's subtle reference to it belonging to Jeremy, most likely so as not to get on to the sore subject of who really had controlling interest.

"Not really. He wants to move stuff around Europe, was all Colleen would say. She told me it would be good for Jeremy as his business could expand into Europe with the extra money."

"What stuff?" asked Rachel.

"She never said," Octavia burst out laughing. "It annoyed Harvey, she'd told me at all. He thought I might say something to Jeremy, but I'm not interested in business. I forgot."

"Are you saying you never mentioned that fact to my son?" Marjorie snapped.

Octavia shrugged. "Harvey told me it was a secret, and he wanted to surprise Jeremy. Besides, he got me a card for an exclusive club. That's where I met Wilfred."

Marjorie stiffened. Octavia, realising she had said too much, back-pedalled.

"Silly me. No, the club's where Colleen and I used to go for spa days: hands, hair, massages and all sorts of treats."

"And Wilfred too?" Marjorie quizzed, not letting the slip pass by unnoticed.

"No. I don't know why I said that. I need the loo. Where is it?"

"Back there." Marjorie's tone could have frozen lava.

As soon as she was out of earshot, Rachel lowered her voice. "It sounds like Harvey Fanston may have wanted to use Jeremy's connections for exports or imports. I'm wondering if his plans were legal."

"And he paid my pathetic daughter-in-law off with a club membership for her silence," Marjorie sighed.

"Sounds like it."

"I don't know which is worse: Fanston's bribe or my silly daughter-in-law taking it."

"As you said, she's gullible when it comes to the highlife." *As is Jeremy,* thought Rachel, but didn't add that fact.

"I should have known from the way she and Wilfred have been behaving that they knew each other before the party the other night. It's conclusive, then: the dreadful woman's having an affair."

Rachel felt it was time to come clean about the conversation she'd had with Ethan in the gym, but Pedro appeared before she could say anything.

"How do you like the wine?" he asked.

"Most agreeable," answered Marjorie. Rachel's thoughts were elsewhere. The evidence against Harvey Fanston was stacking up, but she still had to consider the others before homing in on him.

Once Octavia returned from the toilets, they left to visit one last bar where Rachel got the opportunity to ask if

Colleen and Harvey Fanston had a good marriage. She wasn't sure an answer from someone who was most probably being unfaithful to her own husband would be worth taking too much account of, but she wanted to hear what Octavia had to say.

"They were really close, much closer than I am to Jeremy. Your son can be a real spoilsport sometimes, Marjorie, always worrying about money. I keep telling him not to… that when…"

Marjorie's lips pursed. "When what, dear?"

"Never mind. All I'm saying is… well… he's lost his edge. How am I supposed to go to all the functions the Fanstons attend without new dresses? You can't be seen wearing the same dress twice in our circles."

Marjorie raised a hand. "May I remind you Lady Fanston is dead and you are unlikely to be attending any more of the aforesaid functions. And… before you say anything else that you might regret, I suggest you remember that my son is blood, dear. If you think for one moment I'm going to criticise him in front of you, you need your head examining. I think it's time to leave, Rachel." Belying her age, Marjorie jumped off the stool like a gazelle, a woman on a mission. Rachel leapt after her.

Uncomfortable silence filled the taxi on the way back to the cruise terminal. To add insult to injury, Octavia fell into a drunken slumber, snoring throughout the entire journey.

Chapter 16

When Rachel called on Marjorie to go down for dinner, she was shocked to see her friend looking pale, drawn, and wearing a nightdress. Rachel followed her into her bedroom. The curtains were pulled closed and just one bedside light was switched on.

Rachel's heart beat fast in her chest. "Are you ill, Marjorie? Shall I call Dr Bentley?"

"No, dear, I don't need a doctor. I'm sorry, I should have telephoned you. Shortly after returning to my room, I felt a migraine coming on. I expect it's the stress of the day taking its toll. I can't even blame the wine because I hardly drank any! I took a couple of my pills and fell asleep. If you don't mind, I'll stay here and sleep it off. You go on down to dinner on your own."

"I don't want to leave you if you're unwell. We could have room service."

"Rachel, you know what these things are like. I'm better sleeping it off. I'll have a light dinner in my room, take two more tablets when I'm allowed to, and have a good night's sleep. There's nothing you can do. Mario will take care of me, you know that. Besides, I really don't think I could spend another minute in my daughter-in-law's presence tonight."

"Neither can I, actually. I'll change out of my glad rags into something casual, then eat in the buffet. She can do what she likes. After dinner, I'll scour the lounges and entertainment venues to see if I can track down any of the others."

"Good idea, you do that. We can talk about anything you discover in the morning."

"All right, but promise you'll call if you need me. Mario can put a callout via guest services if needs be."

"If I promise, may I go back to bed?"

Rachel smiled. "Of course. Can I get you anything before I go?"

Marjorie climbed into her bed. "Just fill up my water glass, would you? My tablets are in here." She pointed to her bedside drawer. Rachel removed a fresh bottle of still water from the mini fridge and poured her a drink, then leaned down and kissed her on the cheek.

"Goodnight, Marjorie. I hope you feel better soon. Sleep well."

"Goodnight, my dear. And do be careful."

"I will."

Rachel returned to her room and dressed down. She debated whether to have a night in herself, but was so annoyed with Octavia for adding to Marjorie's stress, she wouldn't be able to relax. Not feeling hungry after all the tapas she'd consumed during the afternoon, she wondered if the wine had contributed to Marjorie's migraine. Although they drank little, what they did drink had a kick.

It was more likely the recognition that her son's marriage was going down the pan and his wife was carrying on with the despicable Wilfred Vanmeter that was making her dear friend ill. Opting to change again into gym clothes, Rachel decided to go for a run to burn off some calories and ease the tension. If that wasn't enough, she'd go for a gym session afterwards.

After running twenty laps around the track, Rachel headed into the gym feeling slightly better, but still annoyed with Octavia. The ship had set sail an hour after they returned from their outing, and was now heading southeast towards Messina in Italy. The gym reception was lit up, but no-one was at the desk.

She bumped into Ethan as he came out of the stockroom, carrying a shoebox-sized carton.

"Hello, Rachel. How are you doing?"

"I'm okay. Just thought I'd come for a—"

A blood-curdling scream cut her off. She and Ethan ran to the back of the gym, following further screams to one of the studios where classes were sometimes held. Ethan pushed open the door and ran in, followed by Rachel.

Octavia stood, frozen to the spot, screaming hysterically, wide eyes staring down at the figure of Wilfred Vanmeter, slumped against the wall, a knife protruding from his chest. Ethan and Rachel ran over to him, Ethan checked for a pulse while lying the man down flat. He handed Rachel a bleed kit from a coded cabinet on the wall; shaking his head.

"I'll call for the medics and security," he said over his shoulder as he ran out of the room.

Rachel removed the bleed kit and wrapped it around the knife, knowing not to remove the object. As she looked at the white face of the victim, she knew it was hopeless and was only too pleased when other people arrived.

Rosemary Inglis arrived first on the scene, followed by Doctor Janet Plover and Bernard, the Filipino nurse Rachel had got to know well over multiple cruises… and murders. The trio headed straight to the victim; Bernard hesitated long enough to give Rachel a loaded look. Clearly recognising the state Octavia was in, he then hurried to assist Janet.

As Octavia continued to scream, Rachel took hold of her upper arms, turning her away from facing the dead man's body. It was enough of a jolt to bring the woman out of her hysteria, although under any other circumstances, Rachel would have wanted the screaming to carry on so she could give her a slap across the face.

"Is he? Is he…?"

"Yes, I'm afraid so. Look, let's get you out of here. There's a kitchen out the back."

"I can't leave him alone like that," mumbled Octavia.

"He's not alone now. Come with me, I'll get you some hot chocolate. You're frozen." Octavia felt ice cold to the touch and was shivering from shock. She nodded, after glancing one last time in Wilfred's direction.

Waverley burst through the door as they were leaving.

"We'll be in the gym office," Rachel said.

"Who discovered him?"

"Lady Octavia Snellthorpe here. I'm just going to make her a hot drink, we'll see you shortly."

"Right," said Waverley. "I'll give you half an hour and come through once we've finished here."

"Where's Ethan? He had quite a shock too."

"He's locking up. I've told him to stay out front and make sure only Dr Bentley gets through. We'll need to speak to him before I can let him go."

Rachel nodded. Poor Ethan, it would hit him hard, especially as he was the one on duty.

She led the trembling Octavia through to the back office where the kettle was still hot. She helped her on to a chair before rifling through the cupboards, finding some hot chocolate sachets that could be mixed with water. Rachel handed the hot drink to Octavia, who was still shivering, but quieter now, keeping a close eye on her as the older woman cupped the drink in her hands and stared into the mug. Rachel was only too aware that a hot drink would not remove the image that would no doubt haunt Octavia's dreams for some time to come. She knew this from bitter experience as a homicide detective, and from her informal job as a cruise ship sleuth.

Octavia's tremulous lips sipped some of the hot liquid from her mug, her hands almost dropping it as she began whimpering. Rachel struggled between compassion for what Octavia had just experienced and annoyance at how she'd treated Marjorie and Jeremy. She couldn't bring herself to hug the woman, but she placed a hand on her forearm, after removing the unstable drink from her hands.

"It must have been quite a shock..." she hesitated. "Had you arranged to meet Wilfred?" Rachel had already established Octavia couldn't have been the killer. Her clothes were immaculate: no blood spatters and no signs of blood on her hands; just hot pink – clearly a favourite colour – acrylic nails. The body had been lukewarm when Rachel touched it.

"He... he was... just sitting there. Are you certain he's...?"

"Yes, I'm sorry, he's dead. When did you get there?"

"We... we had arranged to meet for a workout. It's b... been d... difficult to keep our sessions hidden."

Rachel's annoyance bubbled beneath the surface as she sighed.

"Were you having an affair?"

Octavia's head shot up. "Good grief! Is that what you think? No, Wilfred's been teaching me to waltz. It's Jeremy's sixtieth birthday this summer. I'm arranging a surprise party. It's always been a standing joke that I can't dance. When I first met Wilfred, we got talking. Colleen told me he was good at ballroom and I asked him if he'd teach me how to waltz; we've been practising every day since we came on board." Octavia whimpered again.

"So there was nothing between you? You seemed close."

Octavia lifted her head, glaring at Rachel. "What kind of woman do you think I am?"

Rachel felt it best not to answer that question.

"Look, Wilfred flirts…" Octavia's lips trembled again, "…did flirt, but it wasn't like that. He just couldn't help himself. To be honest, he prefers younger women. He didn't fancy me, and I didn't fancy him."

Well, you gave a pretty good impression of the exact opposite, thought Rachel, but held her opinion back. The explanation Octavia was giving felt contrived, almost as if she had rehearsed it. "Did you see anyone else when you got to the gym?"

"No. I heard rustling coming from a cupboard on my way in. I think it was Ethan. He usually keeps out of our way. Then when I walked into the studio, Wilfred was sitting against the wall. I thought he was resting, told him it was time to get up. The lights had gone out, you see. They're those sensor lights that come on when there's movement, but go off again when there's no-one about. It was cold: the air conditioning was on full blast and the fire door was open. I moaned about it and went over to close the door. That's when I saw…" Octavia burst into tears, makeup running down her face.

Rachel saw a box of tissues on the table and handed it to Octavia. She was trying hard to empathise with the woman, but it wasn't easy knowing what she knew about Jeremy's finances. Whether or not she was really having an affair with Wilfred, Octavia's behaviour had given every indication that she was and she'd caused untold hurt to Jeremy and his mother. Plus, she still suspected they had gone for a secret assignation on the night of the party. Rachel thought of Marjorie. Thank goodness she hadn't had to witness the scene in the activity room.

Rachel was grateful when Waverley and Rosemary Inglis walked into the room, accompanied by a pale-looking Ethan Amundson. His sandy hair, usually gelled to spike neatly, was giving a good impression of a hedgehog out of danger. He'd obviously rubbed it to death, flattening it in the process. He was only twenty-six, too young to witness what he just had. That said, Rachel had been younger when she saw her first dead body.

"Are you okay?" she mouthed.

He shook his head. "How are you?" he asked Octavia, setting off another whimpering session.

Waverley coughed. "Erm… I need to ask Lady Snellthorpe a few questions, if you don't mind?"

Octavia wiped her eyes. "It was awful, he was just…"

"I'll leave you to it, Chief," Rachel offered. She'd got all she needed from Octavia and knew Rosemary would ensure Waverley trod gently with his interview.

"Right, okay. Amundson has told us you had just arrived when Lady Octavia Snellthorpe, erm, discovered Lord Vanmeter. You go ahead, we can take it from here."

"Has anyone informed his mother?" Rachel asked.

"Dr Bentley is going to do that now the, erm… body has been removed."

"I'll say goodnight, then." Rachel grabbed Ethan's sleeve and nodded towards the door.

"If you don't need me anymore, Chief?" asked Ethan. Waverley had already begun his questioning and didn't seem interested in him, so Rachel pulled Ethan in the direction of the door. Once outside, she gave him a hug.

"I'm sorry you had to see that."

"Me too. I don't know how you do your job, Rachel. It's so gruesome and you're so normal. How *do* you do it?"

Rachel put her arm around him as they walked back towards reception. "Sometimes I ask myself the same question. I expect I'll be on the psychiatrist's couch when I'm in my forties, but for now, I just try to get through each day."

"Not much of a holiday for you, is it?" He grinned, some colour coming back to his cheeks.

She shrugged. "What time did Wilfred Vanmeter arrive this evening?"

"Around six. He used the gym for an hour and then went through to Studio 1. He told me he was expecting Octavia."

"Mm, first-name terms, then," she teased.

"I don't do all this lord and lady stuff. Besides, she's friendly, you know?" Ethan winked.

"Yes, I do know. Did you see anyone else?"

"A few guests used the gym at the same time as Wilfred. He seemed friendly with one guy who hadn't been in before."

"What was his name?"

"I don't know. I was stocking up and tidying stuff. He'll have signed in." Ethan checked the signing-in book, frowning.

"He didn't sign in?" she quizzed.

"Apparently not. The two women who were in there did, as did Octavia, but the bloke must have forgotten or not realised."

"What did he look like?"

Ethan shrugged. "Sorry, I don't know. I only saw him from the back and he was wearing a baseball cap."

"Long hair, short hair, tall, small?" Rachel quizzed. "I bet you can describe the women!"

Ethan grinned. "One was tall, slim, looked great in Lycra and had red hair."

"Spare me, Ethan, unless they were talking to Wilfred as well."

"No. They were on the running machines with EarPods in. The guys were on the bikes. Sorry, Rachel, I didn't get a good look at him."

"And you didn't see him leave?"

"No, but Wilfred was very much alive when he went through to the studio."

"Had all three guests left by then?"

Ethan nodded. "Have I missed something important?"

"I doubt it. Sounds like two men having a friendly chat during a workout. I always forget to sign in myself, unless someone's at reception to remind me. Look, my name's not down either." Rachel thought for a moment, deciding it probably wasn't relevant, but it would have helped if Ethan was more observant. "I'm going to grab a bite to eat. Will you be all right?"

"I guess so. Not every day you find someone stabbed to death in the gym, but yeah, I'll be fine. I'll lock up and get a drink once security's finished. The activity room's been locked and taped off inside."

"Was the fire door open before Wilfred went in there, did you notice?"

"I doubt it. We don't allow fire doors to be opened except when the cleaners are in there. Some passengers do go out for a smoke, though they're not supposed to. We turn a blind eye. Come to think of it, he was a smoker so he might have opened it."

Or the killer came and went through the fire door by arrangement, she thought inwardly.

"Okay, Ethan, thanks. Get some rest, I'll see you around." Rachel gave him another hug and headed to the buffet.

Chapter 17

Walking into the ship's buffet, Rachel was pleased to find it relatively quiet and assumed passengers were in the premier restaurants for second dinner sittings or at the evening theatre show by this time. She filled a bowl with salad and collected a serving of Jamaican jerk chicken.

There was an abundance of empty tables to choose from. No sooner had she laid her tray down on one next to the window than Bernard joined her, carrying a full tray of food. He could not avoid smirking as they hugged.

"I guess it wouldn't be a Rachel cruise without a dead body or two," he laughed, sitting down opposite her.

"I'm pleased someone finds it funny," she stabbed a piece of chicken with her fork before placing it in her mouth. Her eyes watered at the intensity of the spices.

"Sorry, it's not funny, really. Poor man."

"Strictly speaking, there's only one body on board." Rachel laughed, good humouredly. "Silly question, but I suppose Vanmeter died as a result of the stab wound?"

"Yes, there was too much blood for him to have been stabbed after death. Good attempt at stemming the bleeding, though."

"Not really. I knew it was hopeless, he was already dead."

"I saw a lot of patients come into casualty in Manila with stab wounds. Graham and Janet agree he died from a direct stab to a major blood vessel, but the coroner will confirm all that later."

"I guess he's in the ship's morgue?" Rachel was aware the ship had a morgue on deck two, near to the medical centre, where the deceased's bodies were kept to be repatriated. Usually, though, the guests had died from natural causes. Her friend Sarah had explained that it was not uncommon for people to die on world cruises, with some passengers fully aware that the holiday might be their last.

"He is." Bernard tucked into his beef goulash. "Too hot?" he quizzed, watching her struggle to eat some more chicken.

She wiped a tear from her eye. "It is a bit, but it's gorgeous. I love Jamaican jerk."

"Our chefs like to spice it up a little with a pinch of some secret ingredient."

"That explains it. I don't usually have a problem eating it back home."

"Speaking of home, how's my dear friend Sarah? And the handsome Jason, of course."

"They're good. Looking forward to the wedding. So am I, for that matter."

"I bet Mrs Bradshaw is very hands on." Bernard's cheeky grin made Rachel smile.

"You could say that, but Jason's got her wrapped around his little finger, so he steps in when it looks as if Sarah might lose control."

"That's my boy. It will be so good to have her back; I miss our chats, although the new boy's all right."

"More than all right, from what I hear."

"How would you…? Of course, you were at dinner with Graham the night the infamous Lady Fanston took a dip."

"Bernard! I can't believe you just said that. You can be overly flippant at times. Anyway, while we're on the subject of the late Lady Fanston, have you heard anything else about the cause of death or the missing diamonds?"

Bernard shook his head. "Nothing new. Graham called the coroner's office earlier today. Strangled, as far as they know. They're waiting for toxicology reports as there's evidence someone drugged her first, but that's all I have."

"At least she wouldn't have suffered if they drugged her."

"And they found no diamonds on her person. The coroner doesn't believe they came off through swelling, but says they could have come off from the fall. Everyone's guess is they must have been stolen, and that was the motive."

"That's what I'm thinking," said Rachel, "but without enough evidence, I don't expect Waverley can order a search of the other guests' rooms. I'm convinced whoever killed her did it for the diamonds, but now my chief suspect's dead."

"Don't tell me you're losing your touch, Rachel? The chief will never work it out on his own, you know that."

"Maybe, maybe not. There's a long list of potential suspects, getting shorter by the minute. Chief suspect now must be her husband. The only thing is, I'm led to believe they had a good marriage, and I can't see Lord Fanston stabbing anybody, if I'm honest."

"Unless Lord Vanmeter killed Lady Fanston, stole the diamonds, and then someone killed him and stole them again." Bernard wiped his mouth with a napkin, taking a gulp of water afterwards.

"You're becoming quite the sleuth, Bernard." Bernard had inadvertently guessed a criminal's identity during her last onboard investigation and he was clearly warming to the role. "The same thought had crossed my mind, so it's a possibility. How did Lady Vanmeter take the news?"

"Coldly, according to Graham. What is it with you Brits, always trying to hide what you really feel?"

"It's true, we're not as emotional as some nations, although the stiff upper lip tends to be more common among the elderly than those of us from the younger generation. A cool response could be because she was trying to put on a brave face, as you're inferring, or it could be she doesn't care. They didn't seem particularly close, and to be frank, he was a pain in the neck, from what little I saw of him. Still, you would expect a mother to take her only son's death badly. She could be in shock."

"You're right. Shock causes people to react differently."

"At least now, everyone will know Marjorie's son didn't kill Wilfred. Hopefully, it will cast doubt on who murdered Lady Fanston and bring the killer out of the woodwork. If it is one killer, something drove them to kill Wilfred Vanmeter against their better judgement."

"What makes you say that?" asked Bernard.

"Because it made sense for them to continue to let Jeremy Snellthorpe take the blame for Lady Fanston's murder."

"Ah, I get it. All you need to do now is find out what it was that changed the killer's plans. Assuming it was just one person."

"The murders have to be connected, whether it's one killer or two. It could be two people working together; I'm not ruling anything out just yet."

"Who else is on your list if you're not convinced it was Lord Fanston?" Bernard asked.

"Thomas Elrod, I'm sorry to say. It would be a shame because Marjorie likes him. He might be working with or without the help of his father. I can't believe it would be Melody Vanmeter. A woman wouldn't kill her own son. Then there's Annette Elrod, who's another possibility. I can't see her being able to overpower Wilfred, who was tall and fit, unless she drugged him, and there was no evidence of that because Ethan saw him enter the studio not long before we found him."

"Hence the question about whether the knife killed him. But you're right: for someone to dope him up enough to overpower him, they would have to use something pretty fast acting, and it would need to be injected."

"There's only one other person who was at the party the night Lady Fanston was killed, apart from myself and Marjorie, and thankfully I can rule her out, for Wilfred at least. I'm sure it was the same perpetrator who killed Lady Fanston."

"You're talking about Octavia Snellthorpe, the woman who found him? Lady Marjorie's daughter-in-law? Could she be in cahoots with someone else?"

Rachel had a similar nagging doubt in the back of her mind, but shook her head. "If she'd been working with anyone, it would have been Wilfred Vanmeter. They were close."

Bernard raised an eyebrow. "Close as in having an affair?"

"Not according to her, but I don't know. Marjorie will be relieved Jeremy wasn't around at the time of Vanmeter's death, although she'll be sorry someone else has been killed."

"Do you think they'll release him now?"

Rachel was pleased word hadn't got out about Jeremy being in the captain's guest quarters. "I hope so. I'd love it if he and Marjorie could have some quality time together."

"Where is Lady Marjorie this evening?"

"She had a migraine, so I'm hoping she's safely tucked up in bed."

***

Noise coming from the corridor wakened Marjorie from a restless sleep. The realisation that Octavia could be so blatantly uncaring about Jeremy and his predicament had sent her head into a spin. She opened her eyes slowly, testing whether the nausea from the migraine had truly gone away. The pain seemed to have settled into a dull ache rather than the stabbing sensation usually associated with the migraines she suffered.

Confident she no longer felt sick, she dared to raise her body to a sitting position so she could reach behind for the bedside light. *Hurrah, the wretched headache has all but disappeared!* She lifted the telephone and buzzed for Mario, who couldn't have appeared any quicker if he'd been standing outside her door, listening.

The tall Salvadoran bustled in to fluff up her pillows. "Did the noise wake you, Lady Marjorie? I told them to be quiet."

"A noise did wake me. What was it?"

"A group of nurses on a thirty-year reunion party. They should know better than to be prancing around, making a nuisance of themselves."

"I expect they're entitled to party; I just wish they'd do it on the public decks rather than outside my room."

"They were also on the wrong floor, you'll be pleased to hear."

"Ah," Marjorie smiled, nodding knowingly. "I trust you pointed them in the right direction?"

Mario grinned. "I did, Lady Marjorie. Now, how are you feeling? Can I get you anything? Do you need a doctor? Should I call Rachel?"

"I'm feeling much better, actually, but if you could refrain from asking four questions at once, it would help."

Mario winced. "I'm sorry. I worry about you, that's all."

"Thank you for that, but you shouldn't. I'm quite healthy for my age." She softened, seeing Mario's hurt expression. "I don't need a doctor and you don't need to call Rachel, but I would love a pot of camomile tea."

"Coming right up. Shall I—"

"Nothing else, thank you, Mario. I'll order room service later."

Forty minutes later, Marjorie had showered and dressed, opting for a skirt and blouse rather than the dress she'd been planning to wear to dinner earlier. She polished off the remains of the camomile tea Mario had brought, but couldn't shake away the annoyance her daughter-in-law had left her feeling.

It's no good. I can't sit here ruminating or I'll bring on another migraine. What she needed, she decided, was a breath of fresh air to shake the cobwebs from her brain. Passing Mario on her way out, she explained she didn't need anything else tonight and actively encouraged him to go for a rest.

Marjorie felt the welcome breeze hit her face as soon as she was outdoors. She stood against the rail for a few moments, allowing her blood pressure to balance itself whilst checking the nausea wasn't going to return. All that remained of the migraine was a slight throbbing in the back of her head. She felt a little fuzzy from the medication, but could live with that.

The ship cut through the dark sea, but it was a calm night, so there wasn't too much motion. Strolling around the deck, Marjorie stayed close to the rail in case she needed to grab hold of something, having forgotten to bring her stick – nothing unusual.

Spotting the tall, slim figure of someone she recognised, Marjorie considered turning back in order to avoid the woman who most probably believed Marjorie's son had strangled her sister, but then she heard a quiet sob.

"Are you quite all right?" Marjorie moved closer.

Melody Vanmeter appeared startled for a moment. Her dull brown eyes were dry even as she let out another sob. Still no tears. Marjorie had heard of women who could cry without tears, but she'd never met one before now.

"I'm sure you miss your sister terribly, Lady Vanmeter," Marjorie said, using the title the woman would have inherited from her father.

"Melody," she shook her head. "Please call me Melody or Mel."

"I think we'll opt for Melody." Marjorie wouldn't be able to bring herself to call anyone as old as Lady Vanmeter Mel. "Would you prefer to be alone?"

Melody shook her head vigorously. "No. It's not Colleen, it's… it's Willy."

Marjorie had to shake the fog from her brain to understand Melody was most likely speaking of Wilfred. *Why don't people stick to their given names, and what's the wretched man done now?* she was tempted to ask, but seeing how upset Melody was, she empathised instead. *None of us are responsible for our children's behaviour. Jeremy can be challenging at times, so Melody isn't to blame for her son's faults.*

"Would you like to talk about it?"

Instead of issuing a rebuff, Melody grabbed Marjorie's hand. "He's… he's…" Marjorie waited patiently, expecting to hear what she already knew – that Melody's son was having an affair with Octavia.

"Our children make their own choices," she said, trying to sound sympathetic.

Confusion crossed Melody's face before she continued, bottom lip trembling. "He's dead. Wilfred… my Willy's been murdered."

Marjorie stared, stunned, at the varicosed hand still clutching her arm, trying to process what she had just heard.

"Murdered? Was he attacked on shore?"

"No. Tonight… he's been stabbed to death tonight. They found him in the gym. Your daughter-in-law found him, and your friend."

"Rachel?" At least that was something. Marjorie would get some sense out of Rachel later.

"Yes. The doctor says he wouldn't have suffered; he died instantly."

Marjorie hoped that was true rather than Dr Bentley trying to reassure a bereaved mother by telling her what she no doubt wanted to hear. She didn't like Wilfred, but she wouldn't have wanted him to suffer. Then a terrible thought flashed through her mind.

"Do they know who killed him?"

"No."

Marjorie realised she'd been holding her breath. Thank goodness Octavia wasn't under arrest.

Melody was shivering; she was outside wearing a strapless dress and no jacket.

"Shall we go inside? Perhaps we could find somewhere warmer to sit and talk."

Melody acquiesced, following Marjorie indoors. "I need a cigarette," she said.

"I'm not sure I know where one is allowed to smoke," said Marjorie.

"I do. There's a cigar lounge. Follow me."

Joy! thought Marjorie cynically. *I hope my head can take it.*

"Righty ho," she said.

Marjorie and Melody had to wait for a seat as cigar-smoking men dominated the lounge.

"You'd think there would be one gentleman in here, wouldn't you?" Marjorie complained, about to suggest they leave, when Melody removed a long cream cigarette holder from her bag and fitted a cigarette on the end. It was like watching something from a Greta Garbo movie in times past. Marjorie watched on, fascinated, as suddenly a man noticed them standing.

"Here, ladies, please take our seats," he said in a polite American accent, urging the man next to him to his feet. "Can I offer you a light, mam?"

Melody placed the holder between her bright-red painted lips while the American gentleman removed his gold coloured lighter.

Am I in a dream? Marjorie thought. *It must be the drugs.*

"Have a great evening, ladies." The chivalrous gentleman and his companion then left the two women alone.

Melody had gone into a trance, blowing smoke in front of her as if it would dispel the horrific news of her son's recent demise. Marjorie would not sit in this smoke-infested room, nursing her sore head, unless she got some more information. As soon as she felt she'd given the woman enough time, she caught the eye of a waitress, who came over to the table holding a pad.

"Good evening. What can I get you?"

"I'll have a brandy, please," Marjorie said.

Melody came out of her trance. "Same here," she muttered. Marjorie smiled at the waitress as she left.

Once they had drinks in hands, Marjorie focussed her attention on Melody. "Start from the beginning. Tell me what happened tonight."

"It's like a nightmare. I can't believe it's happened. First my sister, now my son. Do you think someone's got a vendetta? Am I next?"

How melodramatic, thought Marjorie. "What on earth would make you think such a thing?"

As if remembering something, Melody shook her head. "Nothing. I believe we owe you an apology, though, Lady Marjorie."

"What for?"

"For your son's arrest. I know it wasn't him. I was going to find you and tell you tonight, before all this happened. Wilfred told me earlier… he admitted to seeing your son's tie in the bathroom that night, just like Jeremy had told the security chief."

Marjorie pursed her lips, fighting what she'd like to say about the late Wilfred Vanmeter with every fibre of her being.

Chapter 18

After finishing dinner with Bernard, Rachel made her way to the Jazz Bar, still too hyped up to go to bed. She was surprised to see Octavia in there, having an intense conversation with Annette Elrod. From where Rachel stood, the two women appeared to be arguing. Octavia waved her arms around whilst Annette seemed to be doing her best to look down her nose at her – no easy feat when Octavia was the taller of the two women, especially as she had changed from the tracksuit and trainers she'd been wearing in the gym and was now back in six-inch heels and a dark maroon dress.

"Are you all right, ma'am? Can I get you anything?"

A waiter was standing by her side. Realising she had rooted herself to the spot and was most likely gawping, Rachel recovered herself.

"I'm fine, thank you. I'll order at the bar." She made her way to the bar, keeping the two women in sight, and perched herself on a stool. Feeling for the seat, she couldn't help grinning, remembering Sarah's tales of drunken passengers falling off barstools.

A waitress Rachel recognised but didn't know by name flashed her a grin. "You're Sarah's friend, aren't you? What can I get you?"

"Yes, I am. I'll have a Martini and lemonade please," Rachel smiled back, but didn't want to engage in conversation while intent on scoping Octavia and Annette. She was relieved when a waiter handed over an order to the waitress, helping ease Rachel's conscience.

Once she had her drink, Rachel sidled closer to the animated women to see if she could hear what the heated conversation was about. Octavia had her back to Rachel, and Annette was too busy glaring at the other woman to notice her moving in, but just in case they saw her, Rachel kept a short distance.

The band's music made it too difficult to hear what was being said. Feeling frustration mounting, Rachel blew out an exasperated breath.

At that moment, a rough hand grabbed her arm.

"What are you up to?" a gruff voice growled in her ear.

Rachel swung around, about to give yet another man a piece of her mind for his unwanted attention, but stopped when she found herself looking into the cold, dark eyes of Thomas Elrod. Gone was the friendly demeanour of the man she'd met on the first night of the voyage; in its place was a tight-lipped, red-faced effigy.

The grip tightened.

"Mr Elrod, Tom, you're hurting my arm."

Without loosening his grip, Thomas pulled her towards the door. Deciding it better not to create a scene, Rachel allowed herself to be manhandled, certain she could deal with Thomas Elrod if she needed to.

Once they were in a quiet public corridor, Tom hissed again, "What were you doing just now?"

"I don't think that's any of your business, but if you let go of my arm, I'll tell you."

Tom released his grip. "So?" He tried to face-off with her, but she was taller than he was and it made her want to laugh. Now they were away from the dim lighting in the bar. She could see his eyes were puffy, as if he hadn't slept in days.

"If you must know, I was having a drink. One that's most likely been cleared away following your abrupt and unacceptable behaviour."

"Don't give me that. I know your background. You were watching my wife. What I want to know is why?"

"I was about to say hello. She was speaking with Marjorie's daughter-in-law."

Tom's eyes bulged. "If you keep lying to me, I'm going to have to force it out of you." He went to grab her arm, but this time, Rachel deflected him with a swift block. He tried again, but she dodged his grasp and twisted his arm behind his back.

"Tom, we're in a public corridor. If you really know my background, you will be aware I possess self-defence skills. It might also be the moment to point out to you that I am a karate black belt. Now, I would prefer not to have to incapacitate you, but if you don't calm down, I will."

"Okay, okay," he groaned. "You can let go. I'm calm."

"Are you sure?"

"Sure."

Rachel let him go. He rubbed his wrist where she'd grabbed it and flexed his shoulder.

"The truth is, I saw your wife arguing with Octavia and I'm naturally nosy, so I wanted to know what they were arguing about."

"Something I'd like to know, too. I guess it has something to do with Jeremy being banged up. Annette may not show her feelings, but she was very fond of my mother. Snellthorpe will get what's coming to him."

Rachel took a step back. "Do you really believe Jeremy Snellthorpe killed your mother?"

"I wouldn't have imagined him capable before this cruise, but evidence is evidence. Annette wants their room searched again, but security won't do it. I guess that's what they were arguing about."

"The evidence against Jeremy, as you call it, is circumstantial. For all I know, you were the one who killed your mother, being the only one who was definitely in her room that night. Perhaps you went looking for her; you were angry she was wearing your grandmother's diamonds, you argued, and then you killed her either deliberately or by accident. Afterwards, you planted Jeremy's tie around her neck, took what you believed was yours and stashed the diamonds away before coming back to the party with your impressive distraught son performance."

"If you didn't look so serious, I'd say that's the most laughable theory I've ever heard. Of course I didn't kill my mother. Jeremy Snellthorpe's the one under arrest. And may I point out that if I'd done what you just described, I wouldn't have come back confessing I'd been in her room, would I, Miss Clever Clogs?"

Rachel tried hard to read Tom's body language and expressions, but he was giving nothing away to show he was lying. He was either an excellent actor or being truthful.

"You could have been playing a double bluff. I expect you have a deft card hand."

"I assure you, I'm not playing any such thing."

Rachel tried a different tack. "What were you so angry about in the Jazz Bar that warranted you dragging me from the room?"

He rubbed his wrist again, grimacing. "If I'd realised you could be so rough, I wouldn't have bothered. Seems I didn't do a very good job of it, did I?" The friendly twinkle returned to his eyes as he grinned. "I'm sorry, I don't know what came over me. I think it was seeing Octavia and my wife at loggerheads. It annoyed me. The audacity of the woman, after her husband killed my mother. You were just in the way, as it were. I guess I took my anger out on you." Tom sounded genuinely contrite.

"You keep repeating that Jeremy killed your mother, which I don't believe is true. Anyway, I'm not sure your wife and Octavia were discussing Jeremy at all. I suspect you'll find they were talking about something quite different."

"Such as?"

Rachel held his gaze before making a decision. "Such as the murder of your cousin, Wilfred." She watched carefully for any reaction.

He paled. "What are you talking about? Wilf and I had an early dinner. But he left to—" Tom flicked his long locks behind his ears, lines crossing his brow and panic filling his eyes.

"I'm afraid your cousin was found dead in one of the rooms in the gym, probably not long after you saw him."

"I don't believe it. He told me he was going to meet Octavia." Tom's jaw tensed. "Now I get it. *That's* what Annette and Octavia are arguing about. So, my wife is still holding a torch for Cousin Wilf."

"What do you mean? I thought you told Marjorie it was the other way around."

"On Wilf's side? Yes, it was that too. He hated me for getting the woman he was in love with. They were an item when Annette and I met; you could say I stole her heart, but I don't think I did. It was never mine. I've recently suspected they might have been having an affair throughout our marriage. A man doesn't like to admit a woman married him for his money – or at least the promise of it – but I've come to believe my wife is a ruthless gold digger. There it is… I've said it. I thought I was the winner, but perhaps the reality is I've been the loser from the word go."

"Are you suggesting Wilfred's hatred towards you was all for show?"

Tom rubbed his right eye until it reddened. "Not at first. Annette might even have loved me a little when we married. At least, she gave the impression she did. Her affection lost its spark soon after the honeymoon. Nothing was ever said; we just drifted apart and our marriage became a sham."

"So you find solace elsewhere." Rachel's sentence was a statement rather than a question. She didn't feel sorry for Tom at all. He had deliberately wooed a woman in a relationship just so he could get one over on his cousin.

Tom grinned flirtatiously. "You could say that, but can't you see? I'm the one who's been wronged here."

Rachel shook her head in disbelief. "No, Tom, I can't see that at all. From where I'm standing, you were made for each other: you're both callous in different ways. You because you were playing macho games with your cousin, always needing to come out on top, and your wife because she used you to get to your inheritance. Presumably you waved that carrot in front of her when you stole her..." Rachel paused "...*heart*."

Flicking his hair behind his ears again, Tom glowered. Rachel observed his temple pulsating.

"My, my, you don't pull the punches, do you, Miss Nosy Britches? But you're right about one thing: my wife doesn't have a heart."

"The thing you're missing, Tom, is that neither do you," said Rachel, sadly.

Tom turned away and marched back towards the Jazz Bar, leaving Rachel staring after him. Marjorie was going to be disappointed that the otherwise charming Thomas Elrod had feet of clay. He was clearly a man with a temper, but now she was bewildered about whether it was he or his wife who couldn't bear to be in the marriage a moment longer.

Why on earth did Lady Fanston decide to wear the diamonds on the evening of her death? Diamond wedding anniversary or not. Surely she knew it was likely to provoke simmering rage in one or more of the party. Perhaps she hadn't realised just how far one of them would go to get at the gems.

Rachel headed back upstairs to her room. The depths of evil in human nature never failed to amaze her.

Chapter 19

The next morning, Rachel was happy to see that when Marjorie answered the door, she looked much better than she had done the previous evening. Rachel kissed her on the cheek.

"I'm pleased to see you've got some colour in your face. How are you?"

"Back to my usual old self. Mario tells me you were checking up on me last night."

"Hardly! I called him and asked if you had needed anything. He told me you'd gone out for a walk before retiring for the night. I don't think he approved of the walk bit, mind."

"Hmm, he fusses too much. Did he tell you a nurses' reunion party was what woke me in the first place?"

"No, he didn't mention that." Rachel followed Marjorie into her room as her friend retrieved her handbag. "What's that smell?

Marjorie chuckled. "Ah, that. It's cigar smoke, my dear. I had the good fortune to spend an hour in the Cigar Lounge last evening."

Rachel raised an eyebrow at the inverted humour. "Dare I ask why?"

"I came across Melody Vanmeter on my evening travels. She smokes, you know?"

"You don't say," Rachel laughed. "So you already know about what happened to Wilfred?"

"I do indeed. You must tell me all about it, but first, let's go down to the restaurant to meet Octavia. I expect she'll need our sympathies this morning. Not that she deserves them, silly woman."

They started down the corridor. Considering another dead body had turned up, Marjorie was taking it all in her stride and looking remarkably chipper.

"I had a chat with Octavia after the erm… incident," Rachel told her friend. "She says Wilfred had been teaching her to dance for a surprise birthday party for Jeremy. She denied having an affair."

"Do you believe her?"

"Considering what I discovered later, I could be inclined to."

They paused the conversation as they arrived at the lifts where passengers were congregated, waiting for the next ones to arrive.

"We'll continue this one later," said Marjorie.

The restaurant was busy; it being another sea day. Marjorie's eyes lit up as a waiter showed them to their table, not that he needed to, as they knew the way. Jeremy and Octavia were already there.

"Mother," Jeremy stood, nodding a greeting as the waiter pulled the chair out for Marjorie.

"I was hoping you'd be here. I take it Melody told the chief what Wilfred had told her before his…" Marjorie glanced towards a puffy-eyed Octavia "… demise?"

"She did. It's all in the open now. I'm a free man."

Octavia pouted. "You should have told me Jeremy was still on board."

"Why? Would it have made a difference?" Marjorie said curtly, picking up the menu. Rachel sat next to Octavia; Marjorie was clearly not yet ready to forgive her daughter-in-law's indiscretions.

"We were asked to keep it a secret."

"Not from me, surely? I'm his wife," Octavia snapped.

"Let's not go over this again," Jeremy patted his wife's hand.

"Humph. You do not know what I've been through these past two days," Octavia wiped a tear from her eye.

"I don't believe it was a walk in the park for my son when he was arrested, but you didn't seem too concerned about that." Marjorie's caustic tone caused all their heads to turn. Relief at having her son officially released seemed to have opened the gates for her to vent the anger she still felt towards Octavia.

"Are you going to let your mother speak to me like this, Jeremy?"

"We've all had a troublesome couple of days, but it's over now. Why don't we order breakfast? I'm hungry." Jeremy looked at Rachel for support.

"It's good to see you, Jeremy," she offered. Kicking her friend under the table, she added, "You were just saying how nice it was to spend some time with Octavia yesterday, weren't you, Marjorie?"

Marjorie lifted her eyes from the menu, looking at Rachel first, then Octavia. "Yes, it was. I'm sorry about Wilfred Vanmeter. It must have been a terrible shock, finding him like that."

Octavia's bottom lip trembled. Eyes avoiding Marjorie's, she whispered, staring doe-eyed at Jeremy, "It was awful."

Jeremy took her hand. "It must have been. Try not to think about it anymore, I'm here now."

"Good idea," agreed Marjorie.

Just in time, the waiter appeared to take their orders for breakfast. Rachel wasn't a fan of the formal restaurant breakfasts; she preferred the more relaxed atmosphere in the ship's buffet where she could choose the healthy options, but Marjorie's joy at having Jeremy back made it all worthwhile. Jeremy ordered a full English breakfast, as did Marjorie, who probably hadn't eaten the night before. Octavia settled for fresh grapefruit, followed by a continental offering with a selection of meats.

"I'll have the grapefruit and brown toast please," Rachel said when her turn came.

There was no further mention of murder over breakfast. Jeremy and Marjorie chatted happily while Octavia picked at her food, glumly responding to any questions with one-word answers. Rachel was pleased to see mother and son getting on so well, but couldn't work out whether Octavia's mood was down to Wilfred's death, not being informed about Jeremy being hidden away as a guest of the captain, or jealousy at not playing centre stage. No doubt a mixture of the three, she concluded.

Once breakfast was over, Jeremy asked his wife, "Did you have any plans for today?"

"I was supposed to be having a spa day with Colleen, Melody and Annette. We planned it before the cruise, but I don't know whether the other two will feel like it. When I saw Annette last night, she was in a right mood."

Rachel's ears pricked up, but she didn't say anything.

"What about?" Marjorie asked.

"She'd heard about Wilfred and was pretty upset about it. You'd think it was her husband who'd died. She made some nasty accusations about me and him, which just weren't true." Octavia's eyes pleaded with Jeremy.

"Such as?" Marjorie clearly wasn't going to let this one pass.

"Never mind. Still, she might be in a better mood this morning. Would you mind if I went, Jeremy? I could do with a bit of relaxation after all I've been through."

Rachel kicked Marjorie's shoe before she said anything else.

"Of course. You go and enjoy yourself. I've arranged to meet Tom and Harvey now I'm no longer *persona non grata*."

"Is that wise?" asked Marjorie.

"Why wouldn't it be?" Octavia butted in.

"Assuming none of us at this table goes around murdering people, there's still a killer among said group."

"I've been thinking about that," said Jeremy. "It wouldn't surprise me if Colleen's death was an accident after all. She'd had a lot to drink that night."

"I agree. All this talk of murder unnerves me," said Octavia.

"But you can hardly suggest Wilfred Vanmeter's death was an accident?" Marjorie persisted.

"No, but Wilfred had a habit of getting under people's skin. And taking other men's wives." Rachel noticed a brief glance at Octavia and the woman's face flushed red. "He's argued with at least five men that I know of since Colleen's disappearance."

"What about?" Octavia quizzed.

"For his inappropriate behaviour towards their womenfolk. It wouldn't surprise me if he chose the wrong man's wife for his latest conquest. I really don't believe anyone in the Fanston party was responsible for either death, so we're all quite safe, Mother. Don't worry yourself."

"Jeremy's right. We're on holiday. It's time to chill out." Octavia's voice sounded far from chilled out.

"But didn't the security chief say Lady Fanston was strangled?" Rachel quizzed. Did Jeremy have a 'rational' explanation for that as well?

"It's not unknown for people to get tangled up in scarfs – or ties, for that matter – and end up strangling themselves. As I said before, I had a lot of time to think about it while I was on my own. And as sorry as I am that Colleen is dead, I'm sure it was a drunken accident. If someone did kill her, it was more likely to have been someone following her and trying to steal the diamonds. I've explained my theory to Chief Waverley, who's in complete agreement. I've also given him a description of the men Wilfred argued with."

Jeremy raised a finger to stop his mother from saying anything else. He leaned over and kissed her on the cheek.

"Time to get back to our holiday, Mother. I have business to discuss with Harvey."

As quickly as Marjorie's face had filled with joy, it was now ablaze with anger, grief, and disappointment. She didn't speak for a full five minutes after Jeremy and Octavia departed. Marjorie wasn't prone to mood swings, but her son and daughter-in-law were sending her on an emotional roller coaster.

Rachel finished a third cup of coffee, giving Marjorie the space she needed and the time to recover. One thing she knew about Marjorie was that she needed to feel in control of her emotions.

Finally, Marjorie spoke.

"Can you believe that ridiculous nonsense?"

"No, but I can understand why people would want to go into denial. I come across it all the time. We can't blame them for not wanting to believe there's a killer among their friends."

"Somehow, I think my son's head is more focussed on this business proposition of Harvey Fanston's than on reality, so you're right there. But I can blame the idiotic security chief for being taken in by the most unbelievable poppycock. He knows Colleen Fanston was strangled, and as for Wilfred – jealous or not, cruise passengers don't go around stabbing people at the first sign of a flirtation, do they? Stupid man!"

Rachel had been waiting for Marjorie to turn the focus of her attention towards poor Waverley. She took a deep breath before answering, knowing how distressed Marjorie was beneath the anger.

"I guess the chief just wants a quiet life as well. Or, more realistically, he doesn't believe it at all, but wants the actual killer or killers to think he does."

Marjorie stroked her chin. "Now that would make more sense. Let's give him the benefit of the doubt. Either way, Rachel, I fear the onus is on us to find out what happened and who is responsible. They all seem to be losing sight of the primary motive."

"The diamonds?" said Rachel.

"Precisely. Who has the diamonds? Once we have the answer to that question, the rest will unravel itself."

"You're becoming quite the sleuth since you started hanging around with—"

"My annoying cousin-in-law. I know, but please let's not ruin a pleasant holiday with mention of her."

"I thought you were getting on much better these days."

"Just as long as we don't see each other too often."

"You can't fool me, Marjorie Snellthorpe," Rachel laughed. She had met Marjorie's cousin-in-law the year before she got married, when she and Sarah joined Marjorie on a river cruise. They were complete opposites, Edna Parkinton being a Northerner who spoke before she thought – although that was not unlike Marjorie at times, but Edna was also loud and brash. The cardinal sin, however, was that she deliberately riled Marjorie by calling her Marge. Rachel grinned at the recollection.

"You can wipe that smirk off your face, I know what you're thinking. Now what do you suggest we do next? How are we going to find this elusive killer?"

Rachel was having difficulty untangling the mystery herself. Each time she thought she knew who might be behind it, something else threw her off the scent, such as Wilfred Vanmeter's death.

"I'm not sure. It's a tricky one. I guess we start by deciding who we don't think it is. Shall we hold a war council in your room and discuss?" Marjorie loved referring to their meetings as war councils and Rachel was pleased the expression worked, bringing a smile to her friend's face.

"Yes, let's do that. Hopefully Mario will have removed my clothing from last night. I asked him to launder it to get rid of the cigar smoke."

Chapter 20

"It has to be Harvey Fanston. He so depends on the money from those diamonds to invest in our business, it's tipped him over the edge."

Marjorie had a point, though Rachel wasn't quite so convinced.

"But if what he told Jeremy is true, the diamonds already belong to him. In which case, Tom's the most likely candidate. Here he is, stuck in a marriage that by his own admission is loveless, and then he suspects, or finds out, his wife's been having a long-term affair with the cousin he believes he's superior to. He has motive for both murders, plus he had opportunity and, I suspect, the means."

Marjorie scratched her head. "I'd so much rather it be Harvey Fanston; it would get my son away from whatever aspirations the man has given him, and I don't like the fact he bribed the silly Octavia to keep secrets from Jeremy."

"Granted, he's not someone you'd want to do business with, but from what we've learned so far, his marriage was a happy one."

Rachel thought back to the conversations they'd had with the others from the party. All of them had said the Fanstons were happy. They'd been together for sixty years, that must mean something, and they were both conniving individuals, which made them a good partnership. She couldn't see Lord Fanston as his wife's killer.

"I suppose if he'd found out Wilfred had murdered his wife and stolen the diamonds, that would be motive enough to kill his nephew."

"I hadn't considered that one. Of course, that would put a different complexion on things. Let's assume for the moment it's just the one killer who also has the diamonds. Do you think Annette Elrod capable?"

"I haven't spoken to her much, so I don't know. Her motive, however, for killing Lady Fanston would be the same as her husband's."

"And what would cause her to kill her lover? If that's what Wilfred was."

"Age old jealousy. She believed he was having an affair with Octavia. I'm sure that's what Octavia omitted to tell us over breakfast. Perhaps she was sick and tired of his flirtations in the same way as she was of her husband's. Tom put on a very good act of not knowing Wilfred was dead last night, which could mean he really didn't know."

"But I can't see her being able to overpower Wilfred Vanmeter, or even Colleen Fanston, for that matter. She's so slight."

"True," said Rachel. "Then, of course, there's also Melody."

"She was genuinely distraught last evening. I can't imagine her being that good an actress. Besides, she didn't know I was watching when she was sobbing on the outer deck."

"Okay, we'll park her, exclude Jeremy and Octavia, so we're left with three for the second murder, and for the first unless we add in Wilfred. I don't go along with the random robbery theory."

"I had feared Octavia might have been involved." Marjorie's colour drained a little. "I suppose she could have been in cahoots with Wilfred, if he did kill Lady Fanston."

"As I said, we'll exclude Octavia for now. I still believe it was one killer for both murders. Wilfred was an idiot, a flirt and a drunk. None of those things made him a killer, and if he was having an affair with Annette, he would have got a share of her fortune once Grandma Elrod died. I expect he would have been happy enough to live off his mother in the meantime. His drinking was his biggest problem, I fear."

Marjorie seemed happy with Rachel's theory for now. Rachel would pursue the line of enquiry her friend had suggested by herself; Marjorie had been upset enough already with Jeremy's scheming and Octavia's probable fling with Wilfred without adding to her burden.

"I wish Jason were here, so we'd have more idea about what the security team is up to and what they are really thinking. I can't see His Lordship telling us very much, but I do hope he hasn't fallen for Jeremy's silly ideas."

Rachel couldn't help smiling at Marjorie's name for Waverley; it meant she was feeling more like her feisty self. She too, hoped Waverley wasn't chasing shadows and hadn't been diverted by unlikely scenarios.

"I'll try to catch a word with him later. After all, I was on the scene shortly after Wilfred was killed, so I should give a statement."

Marjorie grinned. "It would be the right thing to do."

"For now, I suggest we call on your friend Glenis to get some inside information about what Lord Fanston and his cronies have been up to since the night of Lady Fanston's death. There's no-one more likely to hear things than the *invisible* butler."

"Excellent idea. We'll wait until lunchtime and then call on her. We can do that – what do you call it? – tailgating thing again. Harvey Fanston's bound to be dining out somewhere, most likely with Tom and Jeremy." Marjorie laughed. "I've just realised how much like *Tom and Jerry* that sounds."

Rachel hoped Jeremy wasn't the bait in some extravagant plot like the mouse in the cat-and-mouse classic cartoon.

As if reading her mind, Marjorie added, "Never fear. The mouse was always the clever one in that particular pairing."

***

Glenis was pleased to see Marjorie again and, by default, Rachel, welcoming them both with warm embraces. They sat in the butler's sitting room, squashed up on a small sofa, while Glenis plied them with tea and coffee. Either hyperactive or overwhelmed by a second visit from Marjorie, she looked as if she would never sit down.

"It's such a pleasure to have you here, Lady Marjorie. Can I get you anything else?"

"No, thank you. We've had quite enough for now. Please sit down, Glenis. We were wondering if we could ask you a few questions about your guest next door."

Having cleared the drinks away, Glenis sat in a well-worn armchair. "I'll help in whatever way I can. It was such a shame about his wife. I only met her briefly, but it was awful about the accident. If only I hadn't gone to sleep that night, I might have saved her."

"You mustn't think like that," said Marjorie. "What makes you think it was an accident, anyway?"

Glenis's eyes widened. "Lord Fanston told me, and the security chief seems to agree. It was, wasn't it?"

"More than likely," said Rachel, shooting Marjorie a warning look. "Anyway, we're worried about Lord Fanston and thought if anyone would know how he is coping, it would be you." She lowered her voice reassuringly. "How has he seemed?"

"He's giving the impression of coping surprisingly well. He actually snapped at me when I asked if he was all right, but he apologised afterwards, telling me that death comes to us all, and at least his wife died happy. I don't think he's as good as he makes out, though. He drinks a lot, falls into bed with his clothes still on. He doesn't think I notice, but I do. His family keeps him company, especially his daughter-in-law, Annette. She's been a rock."

"That's kind of her. Has he been keeping to his room?" Rachel asked innocently.

"No. I don't think he likes to be in there, where his wife may have spent her last moments. He won't go onto the balcony at all, insists I keep the doors closed and locked at all times. I suppose it brings back memories. He did have a party the other night, but other than that—"

"A party! What sort of party?" quizzed Marjorie.

"It was just a small family affair. A celebration for Lady Vanmeter's birthday. I don't think she wanted to celebrate, but Lord Fanston insisted. They were all there with just one extra, an attractive woman. I recognised her from the party on the first day. She was with her husband then, but he couldn't make the birthday party, apparently."

"What did she look like?" asked Rachel.

"Pretty woman in her forties with beautiful auburn hair, very well dressed. I think she was Lady Fanston's friend. She seemed close to Lord Vanmeter."

Marjorie's lips puckered. "What night was this?"

Glenis screwed her eyes up. "I remember now. It was the night before we arrived in Alicante."

Rachel took Marjorie's hand and asked, "Did you see anyone else that night?"

"No, I was too busy taking orders and making sure they had enough snacks and drinks. Lady Vanmeter gave the impression she didn't enjoy the party. Then I heard her say as much to Mrs Elrod. She wasn't happy with her son for some reason, either."

"What about Tom, erm... Mr Elrod? How was he?"

"He was sad. He drank and spoke to his father, but mostly he sat by himself, ignoring everyone else. Lord Vanmeter and he argued about something. I don't like to speak out of turn, but Lord Vanmeter doesn't seem to be a nice man."

Rachel realised Glenis hadn't heard about Wilfred's death, and it was probably best she didn't hear now. It wouldn't do to spook the woman.

"Thank you for putting our minds at ease; at least we know Lord Fanston is getting plenty of support." Rachel felt they had gathered enough information from the butler without arousing her suspicion.

"Yes, that's such a relief to hear. Do you know of Lord Fanston's plans for this evening? It would be nice to catch up."

"I've not long got him a booking for speciality dining in the Steak Restaurant. Would you like me to add you to his table?"

"How many have you booked for?"

"Just Lord Fanston, he said he wanted an evening alone."

"In which case, we wouldn't want to intrude, but perhaps you could ask the maître d' to put myself and Rachel at a table nearby? That way, if he wants to talk, we'll be there, and if not—"

"Good idea," said Glenis. "I don't like him being all alone."

"And don't mention our visit. I wouldn't want him to think we were prying. Elderly English gentlemen can be peculiar about these things."

"I understand, Lady Snellthorpe. I'll call the steak restaurant and do as you asked. Lord Fanston is dining at eight. Would that suit?"

"It's later than I usually eat, but yes. Thank you. Here's my room number," Marjorie handed Glenis a piece of paper. "Call if you're at all concerned about Lord Fanston or anyone else in his party."

"I will. Thank you for visiting me again."

"It's been our pleasure," said Marjorie. "Thank you for having us." Upon leaving, Marjorie gave Glenis a generous tip.

"You don't have to," the kindly butler protested.

"Take it for your family, if not for yourself," said Marjorie, turning away.

Once they were near the exit, Rachel stopped as she felt the telephone vibrate in her pocket. She reached for it.

"It's Carlos. They must have a signal booster up here."

"Didn't I mention it?"

No, you didn't, Rachel thought, tapping the call answer button.

Chapter 21

Marjorie left Rachel in the corridor, having a conversation with her husband. She waited outside in the fresh air, standing by the rail, gazing out on to the deep blue Mediterranean Sea. Even in spring, there was a warmth about its appearance, although she suspected in reality it would be bitterly cold in the depths beneath the *Coral Queen's* hull. The ship was sailing eastward towards the city of Messina, where they would arrive in two days' time.

Seeing how high up she was caused Marjorie to shudder, imagining how awful it must have been for Lady Fanston to plummet into the dark Atlantic Ocean on their first night. *I do hope she was dead before going over the side.* The thought came from nowhere; Marjorie couldn't help wondering which would be worse: being strangled or being thrown into the sea, still alive. Rachel had suggested Colleen Fanston might have been drugged first, which would have made it easier. She had also heard that one would most likely die of a heart attack before even hitting the water.

She shuddered.

"Mother! What are you doing up here?" Jeremy appeared next to her, along with Lord Fanston and Tom Elrod.

"Your father and I stayed in the Royal Suite for our diamond wedding anniversary, and I remembered there is a good phone signal. I brought Rachel up so she could call her husband; she's missing him." That was as near to the truth as Jeremy was going to hear. "Good afternoon, Lord Fanston, Tom. I haven't seen you since that awful first night. I'm so sorry for your loss."

Harvey Fanston swallowed hard. "Thank you. Please, dispense with the formalities and call me Harvey."

"How are you holding up?" Marjorie glanced at Tom, who was shifting from one foot to the other as if in a hurry. Either that or he needed the bathroom.

"As best we can, Lady Snellthorpe," Harvey answered for his son.

"I take it the ladies went to the spa?" Marjorie addressed her son.

"Yes, they all went in the end. It will do them good to have a bit of pampering, what with—"

"Quite," Marjorie interjected.

"Harvey and I are just about to talk over the business proposition I mentioned, Mother."

"I'd better leave you to it, then. If you see Rachel, could you tell her I'll be in Creams? It's getting rather chilly out here." Jeremy appeared frustrated, but knew better than to argue with her in front of strangers.

"We will. I'll see you at dinner later." Marjorie heard Jeremy's last remark, but she was far enough on her way for him to imagine she may not have. She didn't want to mention the Steak Restaurant, or that she'd be there.

Creams was a patisserie where she, Rachel and Sarah often met to discuss cases. It was quieter than many of the public bars and cafés because of a surcharge – one reason it made for a good meeting place. A waitress she recognised showed her to a table.

"What can I get you?"

"A pot of tea, please. I'm waiting for my friend; we'll order from your delicious menu once she arrives."

"No problem, ma'am."

The table was next to a rectangular window overlooking the sea, albeit from a lower height than the deck Marjorie had just come from. It was nicer viewing it from indoors. As she surveyed her surroundings, watching passengers enjoying tea and pastries or cakes, oblivious to the two deaths that had occurred during their holiday, she realised how each person lived and breathed inside their own cocoon, not knowing what was going on around them at all. She was pleased to keep it that way; anything more would be overwhelming.

This made her think about Rachel and her deep faith in God, an all-knowing, all-seeing being, watching over the world, though rarely interfering. Rachel said this was because God allowed human beings to choose their own path. The alternative, according to Rachel, was a God who controlled their every movement and decision. Then they would be nothing more than robots or cyborgs, which would be much worse.

Nevertheless, it astounds me how she keeps her faith, seeing the worst of human behaviour in her job, Marjorie thought.

Tea arrived at her table just as Rachel joined her. "You were miles away. What were you thinking?" Rachel asked.

"About you, actually. What an amazing woman you are."

Rachel raised a quizzical eyebrow, but sat down without a word, ordering a coffee from the waitress who had brought Marjorie's tea.

"Are you eating?" Rachel enquired.

"Oh yes. I'll have a fruit scone with cream, if I may?"

The waitress wrote it down.

"Same for me," said Rachel.

"Did you see Jeremy?" Marjorie asked once they were alone.

"Yes, and thank you for giving me an excuse for being there. I'm not sure what it was, but he just told me where I could find you."

Marjorie chuckled. "He fell for it, then?"

"What did you say?"

"I told him you were missing Carlos, and I'd remembered where there is a good telephone signal when we're at sea."

"Good thinking, you crafty thing."

"I have my uses. Now, tell me what your husband had to say. I assume it was about *old* Grandma Elrod."

***

"I didn't think I'd get you," Carlos said when Rachel answered the phone. "I was thinking I might have to call via reception, but decided I'd try on the off chance."

"I just happen to be in an area where the posh and wealthy stay, so there's a boosted signal. From the ship's mast, I guess, although I'm not sure. Whatever the reason, I'm grateful. How are you?"

"Much better for hearing your voice, darling. Are you staying out of trouble?"

"You know me—"

"Exactly. That's why I ask."

"I'm quite safe, if that's what you mean, although my chief suspect wound up murdered last night."

"I don't know whether you're joking or serious," Carlos said, clearly not amused.

"Serious, I'm afraid. Octavia, Marjorie's daughter-in-law, found him. I think they might have been having an affair, except she denies it."

Carlos let out a low whistle. "Was it the Thomas Elrod fellow?"

"No, his cousin. I'll tell you more when I get home. Did you manage to find out anything about Grandma Elrod?"

"I had dinner with her. She's a charming, though eccentric lady, and a bit on the forgetful side."

"Should I be jealous?" Rachel giggled.

"I believe she was quite the beauty once upon a time – there's a lovely portrait of her in the hallway. She lives in what I can only describe as a stately home, with beautiful grounds. It makes Marjorie's place appear small." Carlos laughed. Rachel had trouble imagining any home making Marjorie's look small, but it was all relative.

"So? Don't keep me in suspense any longer."

"Ah, you want to know what we ate?" he teased. "Would you believe the best venison I've ever tasted?"

"Carlos, stop goading me! The signal could go at any minute. Did she, or did she not, give Lord Fanston the diamonds?"

"She did."

"Not the answer I was expecting. Did I hear you right?"

"She said her son pleaded with her to give them to him so that he could cash them in for some business venture he was interested in. I have to warn you, she mentioned it was Marjorie's – or should I say Jeremy's? – business he named. Apparently, Grandma Elrod knew Ralph Snellthorpe in her younger days and believes any investment in a company founded by him would be sound, so she agreed."

"That means Lord Fanston has been completely honest to his mother, and to Jeremy. I know a little about the plans."

"I guess this information rules out a motive for him killing his wife."

"Did she mention Thomas Elrod or any of the others? Annette – Tom's wife, Melody – Lady Fanston's sister, or Melody's son, Wilfred? That's the guy who was murdered last night."

"She didn't mention the last two, but yes, she told me Thomas was living on a promise. He lives not far away from her and pays her lots of attention – she's quite the attention seeker – but she doesn't believe he will make a suitable heir."

"Are you suggesting she's not leaving her wealth to him? That's a bit cruel, stringing him along like that, especially as he only stays with his wife on her insistence."

"What do you mean? According to Grandma Elrod, Thomas knows that most of her wealth will go to Lord Fanston, with a smaller sum going to her grandson. I think she also mentioned a chunk going to charity and some to her housekeeper, Fanston's childhood sweetheart."

"I see, that's interesting. Are you sure Thomas knows all this?"

"I can only go with what she told me, but her mind wandered a few times. She mixed some details up, but I think she's of sound mind. One can never be sure, of course, and I'm not a doctor. Now I think of it, I believe she would be capable of mischief making, so she could be playing your Thomas Elrod along. In some ways, she's like Marjorie, but more hardened. Without talking to her lawyer, which I won't be able to do, I have to take what she said at face value. Would you like me to see her again and test whether her stories are consistent? She invited me for lunch on Friday."

"Quite the charmer, as ever," Rachel giggled. "What reply did you give to her offer of a second date?"

"I told her I'd get back to her."

"In that case, yes, please go, and try to speak to the housekeeper. Find out if there's anything still between her and Lord Fanston."

Rachel heard a door opening and saw Jeremy, Lord Fanston, and Tom heading inside.

"Sorry, Carlos. I'd better go, speak soon."

"Okay, darling. Ciao."

Jeremy smiled at her. "How's your husband?"

"Well, thanks," Rachel had been at a loss to come up with an excuse for being so close to the Royal Suite, but it seemed she didn't need to.

"Mother said she'll see you in Creams. I assume you know where that is?"

"I do. Thank you."

As the men carried on past her, only Tom gave her a wary look.

Chapter 22

Rachel had to admit this case was becoming more complicated by the day. Marjorie listened carefully as she told her about Carlos's visit to Grandma Elrod and what he'd discovered.

"So that's it. He's been invited back again and I've asked him to speak to the housekeeper," Rachel said, finishing her story and munching on her scone.

"The woman sounds like a scheming old biddy to me. I'm not sure how much attention we can pay to what she said. I wouldn't be surprised if it was a pack of lies. It sounds like she's got her son and grandson running ragged, each hoping for a portion of the money." Marjorie looked thoughtful. "It puts a different light on things if she gave the diamonds to Harvey, though."

"Why would she do that to her own family?"

"Some people are born bitter, Rachel, and some are made that way. Perhaps she doesn't believe any of them give a fig about her and it's her way of getting back at them. There's no way Tom knows about her plans, if they are even true. He genuinely believes the inheritance is his, which leads us to his desire for the diamonds. Do you think he knows Grandma Elrod gave them to Harvey? Because if he does, he's got all the motive, and all the opportunity."

Rachel sat back, thoughtful. "That's true, but that's only if Grandma Elrod is telling the truth. She sounds like what we call in the trade an 'unreliable witness'. Carlos mentioned forgetfulness. I think his second visit will be more revealing than the first."

"How so?"

"Well, if she's muddled, she might come up with a completely different story. And if she's lying, she'll trip up. Carlos will be alert to what she's already told him. He'll also speak to the housekeeper and any other staff he can find."

"And did the housekeeper confirm that she and Harvey were once in love?"

"I don't think Carlos spoke to her; that came from Grandma Elrod. Love rekindled is something to bear in mind, because that would give Harvey Fanston motive to kill his wife, even if the diamonds were his."

"Love and greed. Two very strong motives for murder."

"It's frustrating. We can't seem to exclude any of them with any certainty. We need to find out where Wilfred fits in to all this and why the perpetrator killed him, putting themselves at significant risk when they were under the radar having successfully set Jeremy up for Lady Fanston's murder. That's the part that will crack open the case."

"Good point. What if he told the killer he'd seen the tie on the night in question and was going to tell Waverley?"

"That's a brilliant suggestion, Marjorie. The killer wouldn't know he'd told or would tell his mother." Rachel sighed. "But they would be no better off because their action would also cast doubt on Jeremy's guilt, so they gained nothing." She finished her tea. "Unless—"

"Unless what?"

"Unless they were trying to frame Octavia for Wilfred's death, making it look like she and Jeremy were in on it together. Most people would have headed straight to the victim lying on the floor and touched the knife, or at the very least got blood on themselves in an attempt at resuscitation."

"Whereas Octavia froze. They didn't bank on my daughter-in-law not wanting to get her hands dirty." Marjorie forced a grim smile.

"And she screamed her head off while not doing anything."

"Risky for the killer, though, don't you think?"

"I expect the killer had a Plan B: the philanderer and jealous spouse motive that Jeremy came up with. He's done them a favour throwing it in the ring before they did. Shame. That could have helped us."

"Why do you think Wilfred didn't mention the tie before?"

Rachel hesitated, not wanting to cause her friend more grief.

Marjorie frowned. "I see. He wanted to take advantage of Jeremy being out of the way so that he could have a fling with my silly daughter-in-law."

"I think so, although Octavia says nothing happened," Rachel said quietly.

"If only I could believe her, but I can't. You don't behave like she did if there's nothing going on."

Unless you're stupid. Rachel didn't voice the last bit. "Which brings us back to Annette Elrod. If what Tom told me last night was true, she and Wilfred were in a long-term illicit relationship."

"I can't keep up. Why do people weave such tangled webs for themselves?"

"I don't know, but one thing's for sure: they each have something to hide, and one of them is prepared to kill to protect their secret. We need to be careful what we say, Marjorie. This person has killed twice; they won't hesitate to kill again."

"Sobering thought, dear. You don't think Jeremy is in danger, do you?"

Rachel shook her head. "Unlikely. If anything, he's helped the killer with his hypothesis."

"You still believe it's one killer, then?"

"I do. I can't see Wilfred as a person who would kill his aunt for the diamonds. His focus was alcohol first, women second. Unless Harvey and Tom are working together."

"My money's on Harvey. Tom doesn't seem the type – such a friendly, amicable fellow, despite his penchant for chasing women."

You didn't see his face last night, thought Rachel, but she didn't say so. No point shattering an illusion unless absolutely necessary.

"I wonder if it's worth trying to have a chat with Waverley to see where he's got to and whether Jeremy's theory has taken him in."

"Hmm." Marjorie checked her watch. "Why don't you do that? I've just remembered I've got an appointment at the hairdresser's in twenty minutes, and it's probably best I don't see him at the moment."

Rachel thought that was a good idea too; she didn't want any conflict getting in the way.

"I'll see you later then. Shall I come for you around seven? We could go to the wine bar before dinner."

"Excellent, I'll be ready and waiting. Do try to get that man to see sense."

"I'll do my best." Rachel left Marjorie outside Creams and made her way downstairs to the security chief's office. She hoped he would be in a good mood.

Having worked on how to approach him, she was disappointed to find a quiet corridor and an empty office. The chief could be anywhere, maybe in the operations room. She didn't dare go in there uninvited, so she made her way back upstairs to the main atrium. Perhaps she should just find a seat and read a book.

You never know, I might even feel like I'm on holiday, she giggled to herself.

***

The ship's atrium was a bustling hive of activity, with passengers taking advantage of the main café and surrounding bars. Queues snaked around the guest services desk, and the excursions desk was also busy. Rachel had given little thought to their next stop and had forgotten to ask whether there was anywhere in particular Marjorie would like to visit.

She picked up an excursions catalogue from a rack and found a seat, where she flicked through the pages. It wasn't long before a waiter arrived to ask if she would like a drink, so she requested a sparkling mineral water. The island of Sicily was full of historic interest, it would seem. The brochure highlighted three chief attractions: the resort town of Taormina, the hill town of Tindari and Mount Etna. Although she would love to visit Mount Etna, the excursion on offer was an almost eight-hour round trip, which she thought might be too much for Marjorie. The other two were possibilities, and both had historical landmarks Rachel would be interested in visiting.

As she thumbed through the brochure and lost herself in the details of each trip, she did switch into holiday mode. That was until a pair of muscular legs disturbed her, drawing her attention away from her reading.

Ethan took the seat next to her, wearing gym shorts and t-shirt.

"That was lucky. I was just asking for your room number at reception when I spotted that gorgeous hair."

"You mean you were eyeing up the talent while standing at reception." Rachel nudged him, laughing.

"Maybe a bit of that as well. Anyway, I've got something for you." He handed her a sealed envelope with her name printed on the outside.

Confused, Rachel asked, "How come you've got a letter for me?"

"It was under the door when I opened the gym this morning. I thought maybe someone knew you were a regular. Anyway, I've got to go; I've got a personal training session with an older model."

Rachel thumped him on the arm. "You never change, do you?"

"No, she really is an older model. She works for a fashion agency – good looking, I grant you."

"I hope she gives you hell."

His bright eyes creased with laughter. "As you're out of my league, a man has to look elsewhere."

"Thanks for the letter, Ethan. I might see you in the gym tomorrow morning, if you're working."

"Look forward to it."

A family of four joined her table, so Rachel smiled politely and vacated it, pushing the letter into her handbag. Just as she was leaving, another familiar figure headed her way.

"Hello, Rachel."

"Good afternoon, Chief."

"It's almost evening in my book," Waverley said. "I saw you chatting to young Ethan and didn't want to interrupt. I just wanted to make sure you were all right after the shock of... last night." Waverley coughed.

"I'm all right, thanks for asking. I tried your office earlier – have you got anywhere with that and the other matter?" Passengers were close by, so Rachel found herself speaking in code.

"I'm on my way to a meeting with Captain Jenson. Why don't you come down to my office later? I'll be working until late."

"Great. Marjorie and I are dining at eight, would tenish suit?"

"See you at ten. Lady Snellthorpe is welcome to accompany you."

Waverley was chipper, which meant either an arrest was imminent or he believed he was on to something. Often, that meant he was about to arrest the wrong person.

Stop it, Rachel! she chastised herself. *You're starting to think like Marjorie when it comes to Waverley.*

Rachel checked her watch and realised Waverley had been right. It was almost evening. Time had passed quickly, and she hadn't got much of it left to shower and change for dinner.

Chapter 23

Marjorie had expected Coral Hair to be busy, and she was not wrong. Although the salon was unisex, women checked into a reception desk leading into the female side while men used another. Strangely enough, the same receptionist attended both, who was struggling to keep up with the queue and had to call for help from one of his colleagues.

A brusque woman two ahead of Marjorie was making a nuisance of herself. Marjorie and everyone else in the queue could hear her demanding an urgent appointment.

"I'm really sorry, madam, but we just don't have any appointments left for today. All our available stylists are fully booked," a young man with a dark-brown quiff patiently explained to the troublesome woman for the second time. "I can give you a space with Jenny at two o'clock tomorrow."

"Tomorrow won't do. My daughter's booked a special dinner followed by a box at the theatre for tonight. I can't possibly go without my hair being seen to."

Marjorie, her fellow passengers, and the receptionist stared as the woman fingered her thinning, dry, overly dyed hair to make her point. The receptionist cowered and couldn't hide a grimace at the sight.

"She's right," Marjorie detected a Burnley accent as the woman ahead of her chortled, "she can't go anywhere looking like that."

Marjorie stifled a laugh as the formidable woman rounded on the other passenger. "When I need a second opinion, I'll ask for it."

Mrs Burnley wasn't about to be put off. "Well, love, as the rest of us are now late for our *booked* appointments because you're dominating reception, you're getting one whether you ask for it or not."

Desert Hair turned her back on the woman and addressed the receptionist. "Why do you allow riff-raff on cruises these days? If the cruise line paid more attention to fee-paying passengers rather than the likes of those from places where they take no pride in diction, I would have my hair appointment and you would be all the better for it."

"Aye-up, love, you'd better watch your mouth. I didn't come here on the 'social', you know. Me and my husband paid the same money you did, except yours was probably brown from being stuck up your—"

Marjorie grabbed Mrs Burnley's arm. "Don't let it get to you, dear. It's not worth it. Look," Marjorie addressed Desert Hair, "why don't you ask this nice young gentleman to give you a call if there's a cancellation? In my experience, there's always a cancellation."

"I could do that," the quiffed man said hurriedly, wiping his brow. He had clearly anticipated a fight breaking out in reception and his relief was palpable.

"Why didn't you say so before? I'll take a seat over there, just to make sure you do. Thank you, Mrs...?"

"Snellthorpe," said Marjorie.

Desert Hair glared at Burnley before turning around, making a point of ensuring the woman had to stand aside to let her through to the seats set out for waiting passengers.

Burnley exhaled heavily. "Some people!"

Five minutes later, with brawl avoided, the grateful quiffed receptionist escorted Marjorie through to the salon where he sat her at one of the washbasins, having given her a gown. Burnley, who it turned out was Mrs Blunt – a name that had made Marjorie smile when she heard it, was telling anyone who would listen about the snob she'd just encountered in reception.

"Thank you so much for saving the hour, Lady Snellthorpe," the young man said. "I really thought we were heading for fisticuffs."

Marjorie chuckled. "If you get a lot of fights in the salon, I must come here more often. It's the most entertainment I've had since boarding."

"Ooh, I can see you're a one. Anyway, Charmaine over there," he nodded towards a woman in her thirties who was finishing a blow-dry, "will be with you shortly."

After having her hair washed and permed, Charmaine moved Marjorie to another seat to sit under the dryer. When another woman was shown to the seat next to her, Marjorie turned her head.

"Hello again," she said.

"Oh, hello," Melody Vanmeter replied. Marjorie noticed she was wearing an elegant pale-blue trouser suit, mismatched with clumpy platformed shoes.

"Did you have a restful day at the spa? Octavia wasn't sure if you would feel up to it."

"I didn't really, but Annette felt it would help take my mind off things. It's been a terrible time."

Marjorie was a little surprised Melody had gone at all, and even more surprised the woman was keeping a hair appointment, but she of all people acknowledged the necessity for keeping oneself busy through grief.

"Packed in here, isn't it?" she said.

"Frightfully. My hairdresser told me there had been some trouble in reception. To be honest, I wouldn't have kept the appointment except that chief of security has decided to search all our rooms. I didn't want to be there with someone going through my things."

"Really? What are they looking for?"

"God knows! I almost refused, but if it helps them find out what happened to Wilfred, well—"

"Of course. Do you think they're looking for the murder weapon?"

"No. They have that." Melody turned away to wipe her eyes. "I think they're looking for Colleen's diamonds now that, erm… your son has been released."

Still no tears. It must be some kind of ailment, a tear duct blockage, perhaps.

"I suppose it makes sense to look for clues to see if your son's death is linked to your sister's. It must be awful for you, I don't know how you're bearing up. If you need to talk, I'm a good listener."

Melody appeared surprised at Marjorie's comment, but replied, "Perhaps. I had convinced myself Colleen's death was an accident and I can't say I ever thought your son capable of murder. I suppose the chief thinks the diamonds were stolen. They won't allow me into Willy's room at present. I hope they don't think he had anything to do with Colleen's death. Wilfred loved my sister in his own way. He could be difficult sometimes, but he wasn't a killer. He was rather a troubled child."

"Oh dear," Marjorie wondered whether Jeremy could be classed as a troubled child. He was certainly never easy and often distant.

"Willy didn't find it easy to make friends. The only time he was happy was when we lived near my sister for a while after my husband died. But we moved away to the family estate, then he and Tom drifted apart. I'm not sure whether you know, but Wilfred loved Annette when they were younger. Tom stole her from him. I've tried so hard to forgive her, but it's always there. The hurt she caused my son simmers beneath the surface."

"I'm not sure I understand. Surely Wilfred moved on."

"Wilfred didn't do *moving on*. He was always a sensitive boy; I don't believe he ever got over his broken heart."

He gave a good impression of it remained unsaid as Marjorie continued. "He and Annette seemed to get on well, from what I saw of them."

"That was only for show. Willy was a born flirt, too much of his father in him, but it didn't make him an evil man; just a troubled one."

"Quite," said Marjorie. "It must be extremely difficult for you; I can't imagine how you are feeling just now. Has the security chief given you any idea of who he thinks might be responsible for your son's death?"

"None. Earlier today, he was suggesting it might have been a fellow passenger, someone Wilfred might have upset. He could be right – Willy was bull-headed when he drank, which was all too frequently of late."

"Then why search your rooms?"

"Chief Waverley said it was a formality on the insistence of my brother-in-law. He doesn't believe he'll find anything. Your son thinks Colleen may have fallen overboard that night and I'm inclined to believe him. I suppose the truth is, my son got on the wrong side of someone and paid for it with his life."

Marjorie squirmed, not mentioning the tie and the strangulation. "Is that what you really think?"

"I'm coming to that conclusion. It makes more sense than believing someone killed Colleen, and if someone did, I don't believe for one moment it was any of our party. We all loved her."

"An opportunist burglar, perhaps?"

"Yes. And if that's the case, she should never have worn those diamonds. Although I'm more inclined to go along with your son and the security chief in thinking she had some sort of accident."

"And ended up strangling herself?" Marjorie tried hard not to sound incredulous but didn't do a very good job of it.

"I'm reliably informed it happens. Colleen had drunk far too much, even before dinner. She wasn't a big drinker, so I guess she stumbled and somehow entangled herself."

Deluded, absolutely deluded, thought Marjorie, but she held her tongue. After all, this woman had lost a sister and a son within a short space of time. She was entitled to be in denial.

Charmaine appeared and lifted the dryer. "Let's get these curlers out and give you a blow-dry."

"Goodbye," Melody said as Marjorie rose from her seat. "I hope you and your friend can forget about our troubles and enjoy the rest of your holiday."

"Thank you. I'm so sorry for your loss. Will you be going home?"

"I think so."

"My condolences." Marjorie took one last look at the clumpy shoes before following the stylist back to her seat.

While Charmaine removed the curlers, she stared into the mirror, deep in thought.

Chapter 24

Marjorie and Rachel were being shown to a table when Harvey Fanston caught Marjorie's eye. He stood.

"Good evening, Lady Marjorie. I'm sorry we didn't get to speak earlier today, but your son is quite the taskmaster when it comes to business."

Rachel noticed Marjorie's frown. "Think nothing of it," she said.

"Is it just the two of you dining?"

"Yes, Rachel wanted a steak."

Not being a huge steak fan, Rachel just smiled.

"Would you like to join me? I seem to have a table for four."

"We wouldn't want to intrude," said Rachel.

"I assure you, it wouldn't be an intrusion. I booked the table feeling like I just wanted to be alone, but now I find myself lonely." A cloud formed in his eyes.

"It would be our pleasure," said Marjorie, nodding to the waiter to change their seating.

While the waiter brought placemats, cutlery and glasses, Rachel studied the room. The meat aromas made her feel hungry, and now she found herself looking forward to a T-bone. The restaurant was bustling with life and the table they had been destined to occupy was soon filled with other guests. Rachel wondered why Harvey hadn't been allocated a table for two when the place was obviously fully booked.

"Busy in here tonight," remarked Marjorie.

Lord Fanston gave a brief snort, which was meant to be a laugh, Rachel thought.

"I was a bit naughty. I detest sitting at those little tables, so I asked Glenis, the butler, to book for four, and then told the waiters my guests had deserted me. By that time, all the side tables were full. They had to lump it."

Marjorie chortled. "And I thought I was the naughty one around here. No wonder the waiter seemed so pleased when you invited us to join you."

Polite conversation continued through their starters and while they each consumed their respective steaks. Marjorie had a small fillet, while Rachel had her T-bone, joined by Lord Fanston.

"I do enjoy a good steak, especially on the rare side," he said.

Stating the obvious, Rachel thought, trying to avoid looking at the blood pouring from his meat onto the plate. She wasn't keen on rare meat at the best of times, but with the memory of Wilfred's body lying on the floor while she tried hopelessly to stem the bleeding fresh in her mind, it was making her feel queasy. The only way she could finish her own steak was by watching the waiters going about their business while Marjorie kept the conversation with Lord Fanston going.

The room was subtly lit and buzzing with chattering passengers, enjoying their luxurious surroundings and excellent table service. Lord Fanston and Marjorie had drunk their way through a bottle of Cabernet Sauvignon and were on their second. Rachel was still on her first glass, wanting to remain in control of her faculties. She knew Marjorie would slow down once she'd had enough; or rather, once she had ensured Lord Fanston's tongue was loosened. She had a stronger constitution than Rachel when it came to alcohol.

During the meal, Rachel hadn't been able to shake off the feeling they were being watched. She scanned the room a few times, and every time she turned her head, a tall round man with a mop of curly black hair, wearing thick-lensed glasses, caught her attention as he quickly looked away. Was he just someone dining alone who happened to be looking in their direction, or was he watching them? Rachel wished she didn't have to turn her head to see him, as it made it obvious. She was pleased when Marjorie decided she needed the bathroom.

"Actually, so do I," she said.

Once inside the ladies, Rachel waited for other women to vacate, checking they were alone before revealing to Marjorie her suspicion.

"You usually have a good instinct for these things," said Marjorie, "although I'm not sure why anyone would be interested in us. I hope you're wrong for once. Now come on, it's time to get our pretentious host to tell us what he knows."

"And there was I imagining you'd become best friends over dinner," Rachel teased.

"Never!" Marjorie chuckled. "I can see right through him and his fanciful dreams of using my husband's business to make money for his own ends."

Rachel didn't like to point out that the nature of any business was to make money for the owner, and in that respect, maybe Harvey Fanston was no different to the next person. Unless, of course, he wanted to wrestle the business from under Jeremy's nose or use it for something illegal.

"All right. You go back in; I'll follow and have a butchers at our would-be person of interest."

"Rachel! You spent far too much time in the Met, if you ask me. I know you only use these phrases to torment me."

It was Rachel's turn to chuckle. "Touché."

Three middle-aged women came into the restroom, chatting happily.

"I'll see you shortly," Marjorie whispered as she left.

Rachel made a pretence of looking through her bag for something while the women occupied cubicles. Then she stood outside the steak restaurant for a few moments, peering through the window to check what the person of interest was doing. He had finished his meal and had a coffee liqueur of some sort in front of him, but his eyes were definitely on Marjorie and Lord Fanston. He looked away again as Rachel returned to the table.

"What do you think happened?" Marjorie was asking their host as Rachel joined them.

"I wish I knew. Should have kept a closer eye on those diamonds – I mean, if they are what got my wife killed. We'll never know now, but I suspect Wilfred might have taken them."

"Do you believe he was capable of murder?"

"No. I didn't care for the man, but he was my sister-in-law's son, so we tolerated him. I doubt he'd have the nerve to kill anyone; he probably took them while someone else kept her occupied. I told her to put them in the safe when she was going back to the suite."

Rachel recalled Lord Fanston saying he hadn't remembered his wife leaving the party, but she didn't want to interrupt Marjorie's subtle grilling.

"So you believe he might have been working with someone else? I didn't get the impression he knew anyone else on board."

Rachel remembered Wilfred dancing with a woman after she and Marjorie had been to Lord Fanston's suite on the night of the murder, and that Ethan had said he'd seemed friendly with another man in the gym. Talk about treading through muddy waters.

"If he took my diamonds, he would have to be. He didn't have the brains to be working alone. But we can't be certain my wife didn't get herself tangled up and fall overboard with the diamonds." Lord Fanston rubbed his forehead. "We might never know what happened that night. The chief believes it may have been someone else: a robbery gone wrong."

Rachel was trying to determine whether Harvey Fanston was being honest, but wasn't getting very far. She turned her head to check the table where the odd man had been. It was now occupied by a young couple, and the bespectacled man was nowhere to be seen. Perhaps he had just been eating alone after all.

"But then, who would have killed Wilfred?" Marjorie pressed.

"If I'd found those diamonds on him, I'd have been sorely tempted to do so myself. Maybe he annoyed one husband too many, like your son seems to think, or maybe he chickened out, and whoever he was working with did him in. As I said, he was a weakling underneath all that bravado. That's why he couldn't hold down a good woman."

"Like Annette, you mean?" Marjorie asked.

"You know the history, then? I guess Thomas told you; he loves to brag, fool that he is. He loves her, you know?"

"No, I didn't know. Their marriage seemed to be one of – forgive me – convenience."

"That's what he likes people to think, but it's not true. On her side, maybe it is, but not on his. I don't know what happened, and I don't want to know, but shortly after they married, something changed. Neither of them ever seemed happy again. He'd be better off without her now; they're only married because my blasted mother insists they stay married." Harvey Fanston poured himself another glass of wine. Marjorie placed a hand over her glass with a shake of the head.

"Why would your mother do that? She must know they're not happy."

"Because my mother likes to manipulate people."

Rachel noticed the clouded, faraway look in his eyes again and wondered if he were thinking back to his youth. Her ears pricked up – so Carlos was right on that score. She willed Marjorie to ask the next question, not feeling she could.

"What does Tom get in return for staying married?"

"Everything. Damn woman's promised them her wealth, and trust me, there's a lot of it."

"How does that make you feel?" asked Marjorie.

"Not too hard done by. She gave me the diamonds, and while she's alive, she gives me anything I need when I need it. Not that I ask for it, you understand?"

Like hell, thought Rachel.

"Of course not." Marjorie sounded reassuring.

"And when she's gone, I get the paintings and a generous allowance. Colleen and I would have been well enough off, and with our joint business venture, Lady Marjorie, I have every chance of outstripping even my mother's wealth." Lord Fanston held up his glass.

Marjorie tightened her lips. Rachel could imagine what she was thinking.

"Did your mother ever manipulate you?" Marjorie asked.

"Once. I fancied myself in love with a local girl. Mother insisted I ditch her or she would cut me off. She threw me at Colleen and I basically went along with it all. Before long, we were married and—" he looked into his wineglass. "But we were happy. Funnily enough, my ex is now my mother's housekeeper. I think she felt guilty when the girl attempted suicide and her parents were killed in a car crash."

"How awful."

"All water under the bridge now." Lord Fanston called the waiter and ordered a brandy.

"I think it's time we went," said Rachel. "Didn't you say you wanted to catch the orchestra in the main atrium, Marjorie?" She had noticed a leaflet advertising the show earlier when she'd been sitting there. In reality, it was nearing time for them to meet Waverley.

"Indeed, I did." Marjorie picked up her evening bag from her lap and another waiter appeared to pull the chairs out for them.

"I'll stay and finish my nightcap," said Lord Fanston. The waiter looked disappointed, clearly hoping to fit another group of people in.

"Goodnight, then," said Marjorie.

There were larger crowds than usual when they got out into the corridor. Marjorie insisted she could take the stairs as the queues for the lifts were lengthy. Holding on to her friend to ensure she didn't get jostled. When they were halfway down the first flight of stairs, Rachel caught a glimpse of a rapidly descending shadow heading Marjorie's way. She pulled Marjorie into her arms as a man barged past, bumping into her friend.

"Hey, watch it, Mister," an American voice shouted. "Are you all right, mam?" the American asked Marjorie.

"Quite, thank you."

"Boy, that was close. If this young woman hadn't had such quick reflexes, he might have knocked you right down them stairs. What an idiot."

A few other people had stopped to check on them. Marjorie appeared shaken, but unharmed.

"I'm really quite all right. Thank you all."

"Some people just don't look where they're going," said the American.

More like some people look exactly where they're going, thought Rachel, having recognised the retreating back of the man from the restaurant.

Chapter 25

Waverley beckoned them in as soon as they arrived outside his office. The grin left his face when he saw Marjorie. Shock had set in and she was trying without success to hide her trembling. All colour had drained from her face.

Waverley was over in an instant, helping Rachel to get her to a seat.

"What happened?" Creases smothered his forehead.

"It was nothing," replied Marjorie. "I was almost knocked down the stairs, that's all."

"Can I get you something to drink?" Waverley asked.

"Brandy. There's nothing like brandy to calm the nerves."

Rachel didn't think that was true, but just in case, she added, "Same for me, please."

Once Marjorie had taken a shot of brandy, some colour returned to her face.

"I'm convinced someone was watching us in the Steak Restaurant," Rachel told Waverley. "It was the same person who tried to barge into Marjorie. I don't think she would have fallen down the stairs, there were too many people about, but he made his point."

"Are you suggesting someone was warning you off? I assume you believe it relates to the two untimely deaths and that you've continued to make your own inquiries." Waverley frowned as he lifted his glass. Rachel noticed the tremor was still present.

"Unless someone's taken it upon themselves to stalk old, erm… *older* women."

"And you're certain it was deliberate?"

"There was a large crowd, Chief. I don't believe we can be certain of anything," Marjorie declared.

"Had you seen this man before?"

"Not until tonight. He was quite distinctive looking, I'd remember if we had. That's what's so confusing." Rachel slapped herself on the head. "Idiot! I wonder if it has anything to do with the letter—"

Waverley and Marjorie watched on in obvious confusion as Rachel reached into her handbag and pulled out the sealed letter Ethan had given her earlier.

"I got this letter just before I saw you in the atrium, Chief. I forgot all about it because I was running late," she explained while opening the envelope.

"Hang on," said Waverley, heading to his desk. "Here, use these." He handed her a pair of gloves.

Rachel sheepishly put the protective gloves on and pulled out a folded piece of paper, relieved to find there was no incendiary device attached. Although why she thought there might be alarmed her almost as much as if there had been one. Opening the note, she read the printed message out loud.

"KEEP OUT OF MATTERS THAT DON'T CONCERN YOU IF YOU VALUE YOUR FRIEND'S LIFE."

Rachel placed the *Coral Queen* writing paper into the plastic evidence bag Waverley produced from his pocket.

"So," said Marjorie, "someone is sending us a warning. Why now?"

"They think we're getting close," said Rachel.

"And are you?" Waverley asked.

Rachel shook her head.

Waverley picked up the phone and barked orders. "I need any CCTV footage from the public areas around the Steak Restaurant over the past four hours. I'll meet you in operations in fifteen minutes." Turning to Rachel as he ended the call and swigged back his drink, he added, "Would you mind coming with me? We can see if you can pick out our would-be attacker."

"Gladly."

"I'm coming too," insisted Marjorie.

"Are you sure?" Rachel asked.

"You wouldn't want me to go back to my suite alone, now, would you?" Marjorie grinned.

"Emotional blackmailer," retorted Rachel. "I'm sure the chief would let you stay here and rest until we're finished."

"Not a chance," replied Marjorie, and Rachel accepted defeat.

Once they were in the operations room, where Rosemary Inglis was in charge of the controls, Rachel suggested starting the reel from a quarter to eight. Waverley made sure they gave Marjorie a seat, while he and Rachel remained standing. They saw Harvey Fanston go into the restaurant ten minutes before they arrived. Marjorie and Rachel were not followed in. They then watched an hour's worth of footage before Rachel and Marjorie emerged to go to the restroom.

"He must have got there earlier," said Rachel. "Let's just see if we can catch him leaving, because he was gone before Marjorie and I left."

They continued watching crowds of passengers walking along the corridor and people entering and leaving the restaurant.

"There," said Rachel, pointing. "That's him."

"Blast! He's hidden by that family and has got his head down," Waverley complained.

"It's as if he knows where the cameras are, sir," said Rosemary. She was right. The tall, heavyset man was keeping his head well down, careful not to look at the camera and making sure he remained in a throng of people.

Rachel rubbed her head. "He knew we'd be checking CCTV, which means he planned the incident. Okay, so it's definitely a warning, but who is he?"

"He has to be a hired hand. Someone wants to stop you, Rachel, and they're obviously prepared to go to great lengths to do so, including harming Lady Snellthorpe." Waverley had put what Rachel feared most into words.

"Which also means they're afraid," said Marjorie. "Like Rachel said, we must be getting close; we're just not aware of it yet."

"I wish I felt like we were getting close. But you're right. If the killer believes we are, then we're missing something."

"I'll check the rest of the footage, but I doubt I'll find anything," said Rosemary.

"You do that," said Waverley. "See if you can find this man going into the restaurant and pull other cameras, find out when he went down the first set of stairs. There might be an aerial view."

Rachel doubted it, but anything was worth a try. "If you need me to stay, I can."

"No. I think it's better you escort Lady Marjorie safely back to her room and leave it to us now. I can't have you putting your or Lady Marjorie's life in danger."

Waverley knew how to play the trump card. Rachel would never knowingly put her friend in harm's way. Marjorie opened her mouth to protest, but Rachel took her arm.

"He's right, Marjorie. Tonight was a warning. The next time they won't miss. What would Jeremy say if he knew what happened tonight? We can't risk it. I won't risk it."

"Very well, but only if the chief here can reassure us that he's following some good leads and has an idea who might be responsible for these deaths."

Rachel glanced at the investigations board to see Harvey Fanston's name circled in red. Could Lord Fanston have known they were going to be in the restaurant tonight? Did Glenis let something slip? Why would he kill his wife? Was he as manipulative as his mother? And, if he had no money, why did he think he could go ahead with investing in the Snellthorpe business?

"I believe an arrest is imminent, Lady Marjorie. That's what I was going to tell you this evening. We're just waiting for some financial reports, and, more importantly, we managed to lift a fingerprint from the murder weapon that killed Wilfred Vanmeter. I've fingerprinted the whole of the Fanston party today and we've sent the prints off for comparison. We should get the results tomorrow. In the meantime, I would like you and Rachel to enjoy your holiday and try to forget about this unfortunate episode."

"I'm surprised they let you take their fingerprints," Rachel said.

"I didn't leave them much choice," Waverley sounded smug.

"I heard you also searched their rooms today. Did you find anything of interest?" Marjorie quizzed. This question was no surprise to Rachel. Marjorie had told her earlier on about her chance meeting with Melody Vanmeter and the kerfuffle in the hairdressing salon.

Waverley huffed. "Can I not do anything without you or Mrs Jacobi-Prince knowing about it?"

Marjorie cackled. "I do hope not."

"In answer to your question, the search revealed nothing, but we didn't really expect otherwise. Lord Fanston thought we'd find the diamonds in Wilfred Vanmeter's room. We might never be able to find them, even if they were stolen. They may have already been shifted in Alicante. Lord Fanston assures me they were insured, so he won't miss out."

"So your working theory is that Wilfred Vanmeter stole the diamonds, fenced them off, and then Lord Fanston killed Wilfred out of revenge."

Rachel didn't miss the smirk on Rosemary's face as Waverley's neck reddened, followed by his face. "How do you know what I'm thinking?"

"Apart from the board behind you, Marjorie had a similar theory," Rachel said.

"Yes, Chief. And as I believe you're on the right track, we'll do as you say. Won't we, Rachel?"

"Yep," said Rachel, feeling an uncomfortable knot settling in her stomach.

Chapter 26

Spring sunshine greeted Rachel as she opened the curtains, looking out on to the port of Messina in Sicily. The spectacular view of Mount Etna dominated the background.

Throughout the sea day yesterday, Rachel had kept Marjorie out of the way of anyone from the Fanston party, while keeping an eye open for any sign of the strange-looking man from the restaurant. Rachel enlisted Jeremy's help in occupying his mother without making him aware of the circumstances. He ended up taking Marjorie to an art auction, a mixology class and a tour of the Bridge, Rachel joining them for the last one. Captain Jenson had shown off the workings of the ship's navigational system and, after their tour, invited them into his private quarters for afternoon tea.

The captain's quarters were a home from home. He had an entire apartment to himself and could live there separate from his duties. It was tastefully decorated, but Marjorie remarked later it lacked a woman's touch. Rachel realised she knew nothing of the captain's private life and he had been coy when Marjorie broached the subject.

Jeremy had been bitterly disappointed and dumbfounded when his friend and potential investor, Harvey Fanston, was arrested on suspicion of murder. The fingerprint on the knife had turned out to be Lord Fanston's and, as he had no alibi for the time of Wilfred's death and had been spotted in the vicinity, everything added to the growing body of evidence against him. The fingerprint alone was enough to give Waverley confidence to have him placed under house arrest.

Captain Jenson had related all of this over tea; they hadn't actually seen Waverley himself. Marjorie had seemed satisfied with the outcome, despite the captain saying Harvey Fanston was vehemently denying any involvement.

"Don't all criminals say, 'It weren't me, My Lord'?" she had quipped.

There was one loose end still bothering Rachel as she gazed out at the cloudless sky: the stranger in the restaurant. She hated loose ends, and it had niggled away at her all night.

Carlos had called her early this morning, confirming that Grandma Elrod was very much in charge of her faculties and had definitely given the diamonds to Harvey Fanston. The only thing that challenged her story was something the housekeeper told him. As far as she knew,

Thomas was the primary heir. Carlos concluded that Grandma Elrod was the only one who knew the true contents of her will and she enjoyed teasing her would-be beneficiaries. Rachel didn't like the sound of Grandma Elrod at all.

Missing her husband, she found herself longing to be with him and gave herself a stern talking to.

"Come on, Jacobi-Prince. Pull yourself together and enjoy your day out."

After taking a run followed by a shower, she met Marjorie for breakfast. Once they had finished, they parted ways. Jeremy and Octavia were taking Marjorie to Taormina, the Pearl of the Mediterranean, for the day; Marjorie had insisted Rachel take the trip to Mount Etna, knowing it was something she'd love to do. Satisfied that Marjorie would be in safe hands, she had invited Ethan to keep her company, as he had some time off. He hadn't needed to be asked twice.

The gym instructor jumped up when she arrived. He wore white knee-length shorts showing off his bronzed hairy legs and a flowery short-sleeved shirt. His eyes danced.

"I'm so excited, Rachel. None of the others had enough time owing, and I hate doing anything on my own. It's just not the same."

His brilliant, white-toothed grin made her remember why she liked him so much. He was always so enthusiastic; a young man who loved life. He was also a renowned flirt, but she could handle that. As much as she liked him, there was no danger of her falling for his charm.

"Come on, then, let's hit the volcano."

They boarded a small minivan that took them to the top of Sicily's volcanic mountain. Once there, they were free to explore the area.

"I'm pleased they arrested someone for that stabbing," said Ethan as they set off to take a look around. "I hate the idea of people roaming around the ship with knives in their pockets."

"Strictly speaking, they couldn't, not with your metal detectors. And that particular knife was one of yours, I believe – not yours personally, but the ship's."

"I heard one chef saying they stole it after a birthday party in the arrested man's suite."

"Ah," said Rachel. "That must have been Melody Vanmeter's party. It would explain why Lord Fanston insisted on holding the party when she hadn't really wanted one."

"What? Funny that. I heard it was someone else who wanted the party to go ahead." Ethan took a bite of an ice-lolly he had picked up at a kiosk. Watching him do that set her teeth on edge.

"You're very knowledgeable all of a sudden. Where did you hear that?"

"I think it must have been Wilfred, or it could have been Octavia. Actually, it might have been Annette. You know what I'm like, scatterbrained. I overheard something about the party, that's all, and whoever it was said, Lord

Fanston wasn't happy about it being held so soon after his wife's death. Not that it matters, because he still took the knife and stabbed Wilfred, didn't he?"

Rachel peered down a black crater, puzzled and troubled. "I suppose so."

"Don't tell me you think someone else did it, Rachel!"

Studying the rocks and half-listening to a nearby tour guide telling passengers the history of the place, Rachel was trying to remember something she felt might be important, but she couldn't bring it to mind.

"Did this person, whoever it was, say who wanted the party to go ahead?" she asked as they walked on.

"No idea, sorry. I wasn't paying much attention. If it's important, you could ask them."

Rachel stopped suddenly, giving him a look.

"Except, my dear Ethan, one of them is no longer with us."

"I knew that," he laughed at his own blunder. She loved that he was self-effacing as well as good company. "Now, can we forget about murder and mayhem and enjoy the rest of this outing, or am I going to be on the lookout for another beautiful woman to keep me company?"

Rachel looked across at the sporty mixed-sex party the tour guide was leading up the mountain from Rifugio Sapienza, the mountain hut where their van had parked.

"There's plenty to choose from," she said. Ethan pretended to head after the group and she pulled his arm. "Oh no you don't. Come on, Casanova, let's climb to the top before lunch. I read in the brochure, the views up there are second to none."

***

Jeremy and Octavia were quiet over dinner. Rachel wondered if they'd had a row, or whether Jeremy was mourning the loss of the bailout he'd been hoping for from Harvey Fanston's investment. Although without the diamonds to sell, that was highly unlikely to have happened at all. She was pretty certain the insurance money would go to the rather fickle Grandma Elrod, who would probably be reluctant to part with it.

Marjorie, on the other hand, was chattier than she'd been all cruise. It seemed the day out, along with the precious time she'd had with her son over the past two days, was paying dividends. Gone were the frown lines and the pallor; she was back to her old self.

"We haven't asked how your day was, Rachel?" Marjorie waved away a refill from the wine waiter as she turned to her friend.

"Spectacular. The views from the top of the mountain were extraordinary. We took loads of photos; I'll show you later."

"We? Who did you go with?" Octavia snapped, clearly fearing she might have missed something.

Marjorie sighed. "I already told you. She was going with a friend she met on her last cruise who works on the ship."

Suddenly looking bored, Octavia yawned. "Oh yes, you did. What was her name again?"

Marjorie hesitated, but Rachel answered for her.

"It's a he. His name's Ethan."

Octavia's eyes widened. "Not Ethan from the gym?"

"I didn't realise you'd been to the gym enough to be on first-name terms with the instructors." Marjorie was sniping at her daughter-in-law again, so Rachel intervened. She could see the effect the conversation was having on Octavia, no doubt stirring up memories of the awful scene in the studio.

"I often use the gym, but Ethan and I got to know each other on a New Year cruise."

Oblivious, Jeremy turned to his wife. "You're looking a bit peaky, darling. Why don't we call it a night?"

"Good idea," said Marjorie. "You've both had quite a busy day looking after me."

Not waiting for his wife to reply, Jeremy took her arm, standing. He said goodnight to Rachel and Marjorie, leaving with a disgruntled Octavia.

"She wanted to go shopping, again," Marjorie chuckled. "Thankfully, you mentioning the gym put a stop to that."

"I expect Jeremy's glad to rein her in," Rachel said. "Would you like an early night too?"

"I think I would, if you don't mind. Today was lovely and we saw so much, but it's rather worn me out. At least my daughter-in-law behaved herself for once. They seemed almost happy together. I don't know what happened between them returning to the ship and coming to dinner, but they appeared distant again, didn't they?"

Surly would have been Rachel's description, but she just nodded. "Perhaps they were tired," she suggested. "Jeremy's not had an easy time and I don't suppose Octavia's recovered from finding Wilfred like that."

"You're right. And I don't expect Harvey's arrest has helped much. Do you think Jeremy needs the money?"

"What makes you ask?" Rachel deflected.

"He seems worried about it. He's always tapping me for more money for his, or should I say, their extravagant lifestyle. I wonder if he's got himself into debt."

Marjorie's eyes bored into Rachel. She had clearly sussed that Rachel knew something, and now, as she waited for an answer, Rachel struggled with her conscience. Jeremy had asked her not to say anything, but Marjorie was her dearest friend. She couldn't lie to her.

Then Marjorie let her off the hook.

"Perhaps I'm imagining things," she commented. "I'm quite tired now. I do think I'll retire, if that's all right with you?"

They walked arm in arm past the shops, both lost in their own thoughts. Rachel felt like a traitor, not being open with Marjorie, and Marjorie was clearly still pondering her son's predicament.

"It would cost him a fortune to divorce her," Marjorie's statement came out of the blue.

"Do you think it's heading that way?" Rachel asked.

"I'm not sure, but the time I've spent with them over the past week has hardly presented a picture of married bliss. Still, some marriages survive these things. But I can't forgive her for her behaviour with Wilfred Vanmeter, and that bothers me."

Rachel was no more convinced by Octavia's version of events with Wilfred than her friend was, so she didn't say anything.

They eventually arrived outside Marjorie's suite and Rachel kissed her friend goodnight. "I'm pleased you've had some time with Jeremy. Try not to worry about him. Just remember, he's a Snellthorpe and they're made of strong stuff."

Marjorie's eyes brightened again as she grinned.

"Quite right. Thank you for the reminder. Goodnight, Rachel."

Chapter 27

Following another restless night, Rachel woke, pulled on her tracksuit and went for a lengthy run. Something was still niggling her about the unknown assailant from a few nights ago. Marjorie hadn't mentioned it since, and neither had she.

On finishing the fifth lap, she spotted Ethan opening the gym. She stopped running. His wide grin had the ability to put her at ease.

"You're up early. We're not even open yet; I've come for my workout before we start filling up. Do you want to come in?"

As her breathing slowed while she ran on the spot, she answered, "I could do my warm down inside, if you don't mind the company."

"Always a pleasure, you know that."

Rachel followed him inside and made her way to the equipment room while Ethan locked up again. A few minutes later, he joined her and started his warmup.

"I prefer coming in early. Brad comes in about half an hour before opening and hogs this room. He likes to work out alone, says it de-stresses him."

"Fair enough. I certainly enjoy the quiet of a morning run, especially when I've been eating as much food as I have over the past few days."

Ethan burst out laughing. "You're a rarity, Rachel, I'll say that for you. Most people actually enjoy the food."

"You misunderstand. I love the food, but I'm what Sarah calls an adrenaline junky."

"That I do understand." Ethan stepped on to the running machine and started it up at a slow jog. She was tempted to join him on one of the others, but had to get washed and changed. Marjorie liked an early breakfast.

"When we were out yesterday, you mentioned it wasn't Lord Fanston who wanted the birthday party to go ahead. Have you thought any more about who did?"

"Can't say I have," Ethan increased the speed of the runner. "Are you still poking your nose into that business? I thought it was all sorted."

"It probably is, but I'm naturally suspicious. Look, I'd better get going. Thanks for yesterday, I enjoyed it. I'll see you around."

"Here – lock up and post these through the letterbox on your way out, will you?" Ethan tossed her a set of keys.

"Sure."

"I think it might have been Wilfred who wanted it to go ahead. He was the woman's son, after all," he called after her. "Does that help?"

"Not really," she said, frustrated with Ethan's lack of attention to detail. *Not everyone is like you, Rachel,* she chastised herself. It made sense that Wilfred would want his mother's party to go ahead, especially as he didn't seem that concerned by his aunt's death, but he couldn't have planned his own stabbing. Lord Fanston's annoyance at the lack of respect the party showed also made more sense than him wanting it to go ahead.

While she could understand where Waverley was coming from in thinking Wilfred had killed Lady Fanston, and Lord Fanston had then taken his revenge, she didn't believe it. The man they'd had dinner with was adept at hiding his feelings, but he appeared broken. Despite his attempts at the stiff upper lip, she couldn't forget the dullness in his eyes. It was the same look Marjorie had in hers when they had first met. At that time, her friend had not long lost her husband. The look surfaced every so often when Marjorie remembered something about Ralph or recalled a shared moment long past.

No, the killer wasn't Harvey Fanston. He was lost, not angry, whereas Tom – he was another story. She believed the clumsy attempt – although it had worked initially – to warn her off had been a previously cunning murderer's biggest mistake. Would she dare risk pursuing the case again? She knew the answer: she would, but not before ensuring Marjorie remained protected at all times.

***

Opening the door, Marjorie beamed. "Good morning, Rachel. I'm pleased to inform you it's just you and I for breakfast today. Jeremy and Octavia are having a lie in and going to that awful buffet."

"Perhaps I should go with them," Rachel teased.

"You might like the buffet, my dear, but I don't think you could bear too much time in my beloved daughter-in-law's company. Anyway, come in for a moment. I have something to tell you."

"The glint in your eye tells me I'm not going to like it," Rachel replied, obediently following her into the lounge, where tea and coffee were waiting. *Clearly, this is going to take a while.*

Rachel waited impatiently while Marjorie poured coffee for her and tea for herself. There was no point trying to get anything out of her when she was performing the tea ritual.

With cup and saucer in hand, Marjorie looked up. "Harvey Fanston didn't kill Wilfred and Wilfred didn't kill Colleen."

Grinning, Rachel said, "I didn't know what you were going to say, but I wasn't expecting that. I thought you'd roped us in for some horrendous on-board activity."

"Be serious, dear. You agree with me, don't you?"

"As a matter of fact, I do, but I'm intrigued to hear what brought you to the same conclusion."

"First, it was Harvey's eyes. You must have noticed how sad they looked behind all that bravado the other night. The man's bereft. He's lost his soulmate; the housekeeper thing's nothing more than a red herring.

"Then, there's Wilfred. Idiotic, clumsy Wilfred. I don't believe he had it in him to murder his aunt. He was far too drunk for one thing, and if I remember rightly, he was too busy flirting with you know who. And finally, there's that pathetic attempt to warn us – or rather, you off with the threatening note and the incident on the stairs. That's our real killer and they're frightened, Rachel."

Rachel held up her coffee cup in salutation. "You're very astute, Marjorie Snellthorpe, but the threat on your life remains. Not wanting to sound like Waverley—"

"Heaven forbid!" said Marjorie.

"—I refuse to put you in danger."

"Pah, danger! Crossing the road at my age is a danger. Who cares about danger when there's a murderer out there happy to let a grieving widower wallow in a prison cell?"

"May I remind you, Harvey Fanston's under house arrest in a luxurious apartment with butler service. I hardly call that a prison cell."

"Nevertheless, he's alone and he's trapped, poor man. Next we'll hear he's confessed under some misguided loyalty to his son."

"You think Tom's the killer, then?"

"He has to be. It's been staring us in the face."

"Something has, I'll give you that, but the who just seems a little out of reach at the moment. There are so many unanswered questions."

"Such as?"

"Where are the diamonds, and why would he kill his mother for them when he will inherit the rest of Grandma Elrod's fortune?"

"Perhaps he's not sure she won't renege like she did on the diamonds. Seeing his mother wearing them could have sown the seed of doubt."

Rachel rubbed her right temple. "Mm, good point, but to kill your own mother—"

"You, of all people, know it wouldn't be the first time. Aren't you the one who's always telling me the killer is usually known to the victim?"

"But who was the man watching us? The one who caused the incident on the stairs, as you put it."

"I have no idea. I might even agree with Waverley on that point: perhaps he was some hired hand. We need to catch Tom Fanston—"

"Elrod," Rachel corrected.

"Exactly, and there's another thing. He feels no sense of loyalty to his father's name, which means he's easily bought. So, what's our first move?" Marjorie looked at Rachel expectantly. Rachel chuckled.

"Breakfast."

"Don't be so infuriating. You know what I mean."

"I do, but we can think about it over breakfast. I'm starving."

Marjorie huffed, but got up, conceding.

Chapter 28

The atrium was crammed with passengers taking advantage of the shops on another sea day. Marjorie had been almost too excited to eat over breakfast; Rachel was worried she was going to give herself high blood pressure. It was good to see her friend so animated, but it came coupled with worry and doubt about her safety.

Pondering how she was going to protect Marjorie while they made their way through the throng, Rachel saw the signs for a jewellery sale. No wonder there were so many people around.

Rachel wondered whether Tom was the killer, and what lengths he would go to in order to escape being caught. She wished they could discuss the case with Waverley, but he would just dismiss it out of hand as one of her intuitions when the evidence pointed toward his conclusion that Wilfred killed Colleen, and Harvey, in return, had killed

Wilfred. But Harvey leaving a fingerprint on the knife made little sense to her. Surely he would have worn gloves.

"Rachel, you're dawdling. Do come along."

"I don't know if you've noticed, Marjorie, but I can hardly do anything else at the minute," Rachel complained. She was stuck behind a mass of people heading to the stalls lining the public thoroughfare.

"I suppose you're right. I tell you what, let's nip into the nearest store. We can go in one entrance, and then out the other."

"Good idea," said Rachel, following Marjorie into a clothes store. It was relatively quiet inside as most people were seeking a bargain with the 'up to 50% off jewellery' signs drawing them towards the stalls.

"You can buy all of those things cheaper on land, you know," said Marjorie. "It's amazing how people behave when they see a red sale sign, isn't it? Mind you, I would like to see if I can get some earrings for Mrs Ratton, my housekeeper. She's been so good to me."

Rachel laughed. "You were saying about people and sale signs—"

"Don't be such a clever clogs, we might as well have a look once we get out again. At least that way, we'll be carried along by the majority and eventually make our escape."

Rachel raised an eyebrow. "No wonder Jeremy wanted a lie in, he's probably locked Octavia in the bathroom." Marjorie chuckled.

They meandered through the clothes store until Rachel saw a sign that brought her to an abrupt halt.

"Marjorie, look!"

Marjorie had been heading on past the evening dresses when Rachel called her back.

"Have you seen something you like?"

"Not the dresses. Look there!"

"Oh, you want to go to the theatrical ball. It's on tonight. Who would you like to go as?"

Rachel was beside herself with tension as she stared at the outfits. A store assistant, obviously glad to have people interested in the display, came to assist.

"Can I help? We have everything you need to go to the ball. You can go as just about anyone you want to. Even your grandmother wouldn't recognise you in some of these disguises." Rachel smiled at the reference to Marjorie being her grandmother.

Marjorie took her hand. "I see what you're getting at now, dear."

"I've been an idiot. Come on, Marjorie, we need to go." They raced off in the exit's direction, Rachel looking back apologetically at the astonished shop assistant who must have thought they were off their rockers. Once outside, however, they found it impossible to rush through the crowds blocking their way. Rachel wondered what would happen if an alarm went off. She stared at the fire alarm, tempted to give it a bang, but thought better of it. Waverley would not be amused.

"I realise you're in a hurry, Rachel, but we might as well feast on the atmosphere while we're stuck here. I'd like to get to the earring stand over there."

Rachel was tall enough to see the stand was swamped. She bit her lip to stop herself asking how Marjorie could see it as she could barely make it out herself, but then noticed there was an enormous sign hanging above the stall with the enticing words 'up to 75% off earrings' on it. Making her way through the crowds while protecting Marjorie from the over-exuberant minority who would take no prisoners, she laughed.

"Why do they always say *up to*?"

"Psychology, as you well know. Now do hurry along or it'll be lunchtime."

Rachel huffed out a breath. "I'm doing my best—" she was beginning to wish she hadn't suggested a stroll after breakfast. If she'd realised there would be a sale on, she would have avoided this area altogether. "Quick! There's a gap. You nip in there and I'll keep people off you."

Marjorie giggled, clearly enjoying the challenge. "Right, bodyguard, you do that. I won't be long."

Marjorie's 'won't be long' turned into a twenty-minute 'couldn't make her mind up' session. In the end, she opted for a straightforward pair of garnet studs.

"Mrs Ratton's quite old-fashioned, but garnet's her birthstone so I can't go wrong there." Marjorie turned to Rachel, who was preventing a Spanish force of nature from barging into her. With the twinkle in her eye that Rachel loved, she offered to move out of the way so she could have a look.

"Now you're just being irritating. Let's get you out of here before someone has you under the table." A few people had been exasperated over the time it took Marjorie to make her choice, as she was hogging one of the assistants' attention by quizzing her. It wasn't deliberate, and Marjorie would have been mortified to think she was annoying people, but Rachel was keen to get her away from the black-haired woman who looked likely to eat her alive if she delayed a moment longer.

"I wonder if I should get a pair for my maid," Marjorie said after paying the assistant.

"Oh no, you don't," said Rachel, taking her arm and steering her past the angry Spaniard.

Once they'd got away from the clamour, Marjorie insisted on stopping to show Rachel the earrings. "I'd say that was a successful shopping trip, but I do hope I've made the right choice."

"Don't even think about going back to that stall, Marjorie Snellthorpe!"

Marjorie burst out laughing. "I'm joking, Rachel. You should see your face."

Rachel laughed at herself. "You almost had me there."

"What do you mean, almost?" Turning more serious, Marjorie said, "I take it from all this hurrying, you want to see His Lordship about the latest development."

"Yes, now we have something that will hopefully convince him."

"And you have a plan?"

"I'm thinking of one."

"In that case, I suggest we go to lunch first. I don't know where the time's gone, but I can't face that man on an empty stomach."

"And I can't face a three-course lunch, so it's the buffet or nothing." Rachel stood her ground, arms folded.

"Agreed," said Marjorie, pressing the button to summon the lift. Rachel couldn't help grinning as she followed her into a full compartment.

***

Waverley and Rosemary were in the security chief's office when they finally got there. With food inside her, Marjorie was in as much of a hurry to see Waverley as Rachel was.

Rachel knocked as the security officers hadn't noticed them, being in a deep discussion about something. Waverley lifted his head, clearly annoyed at being disturbed, but when he saw who was there, he came to the door smiling.

"Good afternoon. I expect you're wanting to know if we've got anywhere in tracking down that fellow who may have been watching you."

Rachel detected a hint of disbelief in Waverley's tone. "We have some news on that front," she said.

Waverley frowned, which was likely to get Marjorie's hackles up. And it succeeded.

"Are you going to keep us standing out here in the corridor, or do you want to know what we've found out?"

The chief coughed. "Erm… sorry, ladies. Do come in. Inglis and I were just discussing the Fanston case, as it happens."

Once they were all seated and Waverley had requested tea be brought up from the kitchen, Rachel began.

"You said you were discussing the case. Are you having doubts?"

"I'll let Inglis explain; she's the one who's been doing some more digging."

Rosemary blushed. "It's just that Lord Fanston has been so upset about the death of his wife and his nephew. He denies having anything to do with either death—"

"Now he's convinced Inglis we've got the wrong man," Waverley interrupted.

"It's more than that, sir. Glenis, the butler, says he was in his room the night Wilfred was murdered, and the person who thought they saw him near the gym is having doubts."

"But the butler can't swear he was there all evening," added Waverley.

Rosemary looked down at her hands, and then up at Rachel. "She served him dinner in his room and he said not to disturb him, that he wanted a quiet night. When she went to collect the tray from outside, she thinks she heard him speaking on the telephone."

"But it could equally have been the radio or the television," said Waverley.

"Have you checked his call record?" Rachel quizzed.

"He made no calls from his room, but we don't record incoming calls. Inglis has checked all the other party members' calls and none of them dialled his room. And before you ask, there were no calls via reception."

"What about his mobile?" asked Marjorie. "Surely he has one; even I have one, although I hardly ever have it with me," she chuckled.

"He does have one," said Waverley, exasperated. "But he's refusing to allow us to examine it." Waverley rolled his eyes. "He insists his word as a gentleman should be enough."

"If only that were the case nowadays. Although, he is of the age when one's word is one's bond," said Marjorie. "I believe if he was guilty, he would confess it. His wife's dead, he's taken revenge. What else could he lose? He would stand every chance of getting a sympathetic judge and jury. Crime of passion and all that."

"Except someone premeditated this murder," said Rachel.

"Exactly," agreed Waverley,

"I am with Marjorie in the belief he would confess if he were guilty, though. We've both concluded that he didn't kill Wilfred."

"Neither did Wilfred kill Lady Fanston," added Marjorie, sticking her chin out, daring Waverley to argue.

Rosemary gave Rachel a sly smile, out of sight of her boss.

Waverley sighed heavily. "And what brings you to this conclusion? Apart from Rachel's infamous gut, that is."

Rachel nudged Marjorie not to take the bait. "You know there's a theatrical ball tonight?"

"What's that got to do with anything?" Waverley snapped.

"Everything, Chief, everything. That's when our killer will make their next move," Marjorie said. "The spider will come out of her lair."

"Her! Why her?"

"The killer has duped us from the outset. This melodramatic scheming has been the act of a woman."

"But it was a man who was watching you the other night," said Rosemary.

"No. It was a woman, cleverly disguised as a man. A woman wearing items brought from one of your very own shops," Rachel stated.

Waverley's mouth dropped open. "The 'master of disguise' displays for tonight's ball, you mean? In that case, we'll have them. It won't be hard to do a trace on who purchased the items in question."

Rachel shook her head. "Harder than you think, for two reasons."

Waverley looked distraught. "Enlighten me."

"Don't upset yourself, Chief," said Marjorie. "I made the same argument over lunch, but I think you'll agree Rachel's right."

"Right about what?" he snapped, looking at Rachel.

"The missing cruise card?" suggested Rosemary.

"Exactly." Rachel was pleased Rosemary was on the same page. "I'm sure whoever made the purchase would have used Lady Fanston's card. They didn't find it on the night she went missing – no doubt a ruse at the time to make us all believe she had gone shopping, but when the going got tough, the killer risked using it. The card won't have been cancelled. And even if the person used their own card, we could only accuse them of watching us eating steak and possibly running down the stairs too fast. They could argue they were testing out their disguise for the ball."

"You're right, of course," said Waverley. "We will confirm the card used, though, and if it was the late Lady Fanston's, the damned thing will be cancelled forthwith."

"Now, now, Chief. Language," said Marjorie.

"I apologise, Lady Marjorie, Rachel," Waverley's neck reddened as it did whenever he was angry or embarrassed. "Are you going to educate me on who did it and what you think their next move is?"

"Ah, the whodunnit part. I love this bit," said Marjorie.

"Unfortunately, I can't say who it is for sure. I merely have my suspicions."

"But if it is a woman, it's either Annette Elrod or Melody Vanmeter," Marjorie added.

"And I believe the motive is Grandma Elrod's money, so their next move will be to kill Tom at tonight's ball while in disguise," said Rachel. "But my guess is that this time, the disguise won't have been purchased on board the ship."

"We searched the cabins."

"I doubt you were looking for clothes," Rachel argued. "Anyway, I expect these clothes were hidden among Wilfred's belongings, to be removed again after the search."

"No-one's been allowed in that room," said Waverley.

"But it's not guarded. We checked before coming here. Anyone could have got in. I bet you didn't find his key card among his belongings?"

"For once, you're wrong. There was a card." Waverley sounded triumphant.

"When you check, I'm sure you'll find it was Colleen Fanston's room card, taken by the killer on the night of her murder," Rachel replied, steadily.

Waverley ran his hand through his thinning hair, looking helplessly around. "And her cruise card was used to purchase a disguise."

"Yep. That's how cleverly planned this whole thing has been. They bought the disguise before they killed Wilfred."

Waverley sighed heavily. "I take it you have a plan?"

"I do," said Rachel, explaining what she and Marjorie had discussed over lunch.

Chapter 29

The *Coral News* had provided details of the theatrical ball, which was an opportunity for passengers to exercise their thespian skills and dress up as anyone they wanted to. Examples included famous detectives, superheroes, or any disguise that would render them unrecognisable to those around them. It was a clever ploy to get those such as Rachel and Marjorie, who hadn't known of the event prior to boarding, to purchase or hire disguises offered in the onboard clothes shop.

The entertainment team would select three winners. First prize included an evening in a private theatre box for the last night of the cruise and an invitation to meet the senior officers personally with photo opportunities. Second prize included a spa treatment and third prize a choice of speciality dining without the surcharge.

"I'd be tempted to compete if they were offering a shore excursion," said Marjorie.

"Perhaps as well they're not, then. I need your mind focussed on capturing a killer," teased Rachel. She and Marjorie had scrabbled around, choosing outfits for the evening in the clothes shop for hours, mainly because of Marjorie enjoying herself too much and wanting to try on multiple disguises. Waverley had made sure they were given credits to pay for anything they bought; the items for hire were so limited by the time they got around to shopping, it left them with little choice but to purchase.

That evening, Rachel arrived at Marjorie's door feeling like an idiot, wearing a rubber mask that made her face appear twice its usual size. A brown permed wig framed the puffy face, the padded clothing she had chosen, completing the image of a plump woman in her fifties.

Her own outfit had convinced Rachel that whoever attacked Marjorie on the stairs had made themselves appear overweight and had cleverly played the part of a tall male. Even if they had been spotted on CCTV, they would have been unrecognisable. Melody was the taller of the two suspects, but Rachel had discovered padded shoes in the shop which would make a person appear taller than they were, so she was still undecided as to which of the two women was the killer. It could still turn out to be Tom, but she didn't think so.

Marjorie looked perfect as she answered her door in clothing that made her look taller and frumpish. She wore a Mac and a storm hat to complete her disguise.

"I wouldn't know it was you from a distance," Rachel said. Marjorie had refused to wear a rubber face mask as it would have been too harsh on her skin, but a wig, the change of height, thick makeup and the hat did the trick.

"And what about you? You're a sight if ever I saw one. If you'd gone for a light-brown perm, you'd be a perfect Jessica Fletcher. I hope we'll be told what the others are wearing or we'll be no wiser."

"That's all been taken care of. Waverley's had spy cams placed opposite each of their rooms. I've told him what we're wearing. We're to go straight to the bar when we get in and Rosemary will slip us a note. He and his team will be in disguise so as not to alert the killer."

"It's an elaborate plan, Rachel. I hope you're right about the modus operandi in this instance."

"I have to be," she said. She had worked out that this time, the killer would need to make the death look natural, using something to make it appear as though Tom – if she was right about the intended victim – was having a health crisis such as a heart attack. Either that, or – and this she felt was the more likely – they would kill Tom after planting evidence on another person, no doubt with some motive for the killing all ready to postulate after the event had taken place.

"And Tom knows nothing of this?"

"We can't risk him giving the game away. If the killer thinks he knows something, they might choose another place, and if they're desperate, they'll succeed."

Rachel's heart was pounding as she entered the ballroom, doubt creeping in. What if she was wrong about the killer being one of the women? Happy chattering, live music and a packed room made her want to run away and hide. There was so much riding on her being right. One mistake and she'd have a death on her conscience.

As soon as they arrived at the crowded bar, a waiter appeared, offering them cocktails on a tray. Rachel took the piece of paper made to look like a receipt and studied it. She stared in disbelief.

"What is it?" asked Marjorie. Rachel handed her the slip of paper. "Overconfident, then. I didn't imagine—" her voice trailed off as Rachel nudged her.

Their assailant from the other evening approached the bar, but thankfully gave no impression of recognising them. Waverley had filled Jeremy in on the plan and asked him to let it be known to the Fanston party that Marjorie and Rachel were going to the cinema before dining at the Chinese restaurant. They didn't want the killer to know they would be in the room.

"It worked. They don't suspect," Marjorie whispered.

"Eight o'clock, there's the other one," said Rachel.

Marjorie checked the clock on the wall. "It's eight-thirty."

"Not that eight o'clock, silly," Rachel whispered.

"Oh. Now I'm with you. Yes, I see them, but where's Tom?"

"Coming in now," said Rachel. They both turned to watch the small man entering the room, dressed as a musketeer. He hadn't had to do much with his hair but let it hang loose.

"Goodness, this would be so funny if we weren't on murder watch," Marjorie chuckled. Rachel noticed the Incredible Hulk keeping relatively close to Tom.

"That's Rosemary." She nodded towards the green superhero.

"How do you know?"

"I recognise the torso and biceps, they're the real thing."

"Now what?"

"You stay here and watch from a safe distance. I'm on our killer."

The man, or rather woman from the other night, was making her way to the other two. She wasn't wasting any time. Rachel heard her address Tom.

"Your ruff is a little loose, let's straighten it for you. You take that side and I'll take this," she said to Tom's companion, who was dressed as a cowgirl. As both women placed their hands around the back of Tom's neck, Rachel moved swiftly, grabbing the hands of one of them, exposing a simple device that looked like a lipstick. She suspected it was lethal. Rosemary had grabbed the other woman's hands. The woman dressed as a man struggled with Rachel, who had to take her legs out from under her and pin her to the ground.

"What's going on?" screamed Tom. "Leave them alone."

Waverley appeared in a Colombo outfit and revealed his identity. "Let's go outside, shall we?" He waved to security guards near the door to clear the decks and handed Rachel a pair of cuffs. "You can do the honours."

The odd group was escorted out of the ballroom and into a nearby office, watched by a small crowd who had witnessed the scene.

"All part of the show," explained Marjorie as she followed them out of the room, laughing.

As soon as they were in another room, Tom yelled at Waverley. "I demand to know what's going on. Why have you handcuffed my aunt?"

"This isn't your aunt," said Rachel, pulling off the face mask. "This is your wife."

Annette's flaming eyes spilled out hatred. "You killed Wilfred! He was the love of my life. I should never have married you. Why did you have to kill him?"

"Have you gone mad? I didn't kill Wilf. According to the chief here, Father killed him because he killed Mother."

The cowgirl piped up. "Would you tell this Hulk thing to let go of me?" she squawked. "I'd like to go to my room now. All this excitement is too much for an old lady."

"You're going nowhere," said Rachel, who had inspected the device taken from Annette. "Melody Vanmeter – she's your killer, Chief. Check her pockets."

Rosemary held Melody Vanmeter tightly while Waverley did as Rachel suggested, pulling out a device identical to the one in Annette's hand. He took the device apart, revealing a tiny syringe attached to a needle.

"So what's that in Mrs Elrod's hand?" asked Waverley.

Rachel pulled it apart, and it let off a screeching siren. "An attack alarm. I suspect Melody had persuaded her to initiate the ruse and release the siren to embarrass Tom or something like that."

"Would someone please explain to me in simple terms what's going on?" Tom flopped on to a chair, looking as unlike a musketeer as it was possible to get.

"I'll leave the explanations to Rachel," said Waverley. "I'm almost as confused as you are."

Rachel pulled off her mask, and Marjorie took off her wig. Melody Vanmeter glared at them both.

"Your aunt is a scheming murderer," said Rachel to Tom. "First, she killed your mother, stealing the diamonds she was wearing before helping her overboard. I believe she went to your parents' suite by arrangement on the pretext of having a sisterly chat and a glass of champagne with your mother. Was the drink spiked?" she checked with Waverley.

"The coroner found traces of a sedative. I only got the report today."

Rachel continued. "She spiked the drink so your mother wouldn't know very much about what happened afterwards; that was the only kind thing she did. Most likely, on the way in, she saw Jeremy's distinctive tie and used it to strangle her, hoping to pin the blame on Jeremy. Am I right so far?" Rachel looked at Melody, who snarled back.

"You can't prove any of this."

"Her plan was to sell the diamonds in Athens when we dock tomorrow. The next part is the saddest bit of this whole debacle. Wilfred remembered seeing the tie and confessed this to his mother. At first, she persuaded him not to say anything, convincing him that he could continue his flirtation with Octavia, Jeremy's wife. Although he was in love with Annette, he couldn't help himself when it came to women and his mother knew this.

"But alas, unlike his mother, Wilfred had a conscience and told her he was going to let the security team know what he remembered, not wishing to see an innocent man accused of murder. I doubt he suspected his mother of killing Lady Fanston; he more likely thought it was Tom. Melody probably insisted that before he do so, they should first enjoy her birthday party, then he could have a fun day out with Octavia while Jeremy remained out of the way. Melody told Marjorie that Lord Fanston had insisted on going ahead with the party, but Ethan, who works in the gym, heard someone saying Lord Fanston was actually furious as he felt it was disrespectful."

"That was me," Annette said. "I told Wilfred and asked him to get Melody to call it off."

"Anyway, the party went ahead, and Melody managed to acquire the knife used to carve the cake just as she had acquired the tie. She most likely lifted a glass used by Lord Fanston during the party, and later transferred one of his fingerprints on to the knife. Your shop is selling sample fingerprinting kits, Chief."

Waverley flushed purple. "Not for much longer," he said.

"You killed my mother and your own son for money?" Tom stared at Melody in disbelief.

"You do not know what it's like, living on the breadline. I have a title, but nothing to show for it. All the money was going your way and my sister would have everything. I had nothing."

Tom groaned. "You had your son. You could have asked for money, I'd have given you a loan."

"What am I meant to do with a loan? I am Lady Melody Vanmeter. I should be living in luxury; instead, I live in a draughty old house."

"But how did she manage to kill Lord Vanmeter?" asked Waverley.

"Both she and her son smoked, so she knew he would leave the fire escape door open when meeting Octavia. My guess is she pretended to want a word and took him by surprise," said Rachel.

"Why was she going to kill me?" Tom turned to Rachel.

"Once she'd killed her son and seen how her plan to incriminate your father had worked, she played on the fact that you had an unhappy marriage. She convinced Annette that you had killed Wilfred and your mother, most likely in partnership with your father, and gave her the attack alarm to carry at all times in case you tried to kill her. Am I right?" Rachel turned to Annette and removed the handcuffs from her. Annette nodded, tears running down her face.

"I've been gripping it all day. And you're right, she told me to pretend to straighten his ruff and we would set them off in his ears to teach him a lesson. I was going to leave him at the end of the cruise."

"She would have killed Tom with hers and switched devices with you, letting you take the blame for his death, and then who would be left to inherit the Fanston home in London and any wealth that went with it? Tom would be dead and there are no other living relatives. You never know, she might even have tried to get Grandma Elrod to leave her fortune to the poor victim who had lost her sister and son to her evil offspring. No doubt if that didn't work, she would have brought emotional blackmail into the equation knowing the old lady had employed the housekeeper, Lord Fanston's first love, out of guilt after separating them."

"But wasn't it Annette who attacked me the other night?" said Marjorie. "She's the one wearing the man's outfit."

Annette's eyes widened. "What?"

"All part of Melody Vanmeter's deception. She switched disguises, knowing we would have been likely to give a description to security."

Annette launched herself at Melody, grabbing her by the throat. "Why, you evil witch—"

Rosemary deftly separated the two women and Annette fell on to a chair, sobbing.

"This is all supposition, you can't prove any of it," but Melody's voice cracked, less confident than it had been earlier.

"We have the device, and we have a lot of witnesses who will corroborate who said what, and when. All we need now is the diamonds," said Waverley. "Are you certain they're still on board, Rachel?"

"Yep."

"We'll find them."

"You can't find what I don't have," Melody cackled. "As for that," she inclined her head to the device Rosemary was still holding, "Annette gave it to me. I thought it was an attack alarm."

Annette's eyes looked up at Waverley, pleading. "She's lying."

"Give it up, Aunt Melody." Tom's voice was filled with emotion. "Where are the diamonds?"

Melody shrugged her shoulders, grinning. "I don't know."

"I know where they are," said Marjorie, locking eyes with the other woman.

"What would you know? You're just a dotty old biddy."

Rachel resisted the urge to jump to Marjorie's defence. She would have loved to do what Annette had done moments ago, dragging the information out of the woman.

"Such large heels she wears, wouldn't you say? She hasn't removed those platforms since we boarded. They are such a mismatch with her evening gowns and other clothes. She is so elegantly dressed in every other way, I've been wondering what possesses such a fashion-conscious woman to wear them."

Melody's eyes at that moment could have burned through ice. "They support my feet."

"We'll see about that." Waverley nodded to Rosemary, who eased Melody into a chair while Rachel removed her shoes. Rachel turned the heel, and it clicked, releasing itself from the shoe. Inside the large heel, diamonds were packed closely together, no longer on a chain, but securely in place. Rachel did the same with the other heel, revealing the rest of the diamonds.

"Well, well. Not bad for a dotty old biddy," chuckled Marjorie, winking at Rachel.

"Melody Vanmeter, you're under arrest for the murders of Colleen Fanston, Wilfred Vanmeter, for the attempted murder of Thomas Elrod and for the theft of a diamond necklace and earrings. I'll keep these as evidence for now, Mr Elrod, but you can tell your father he is a free man. The diamonds will be released to him as soon as the authorities allow. Thank you again, Rachel. I bid you all goodnight."

Waverley left the room with Rosemary Inglis and Melody Vanmeter, the latter woman in handcuffs.

"I think we should leave too, Rachel. I expect these two have things to talk about."

Rachel nodded, turning to Tom. "I'm so sorry about you mother and cousin. At least you know your father's innocent." Then the two friends left arm in arm and headed upstairs for a nightcap.

Chapter 30

Athens had been bright and sunny, just like Rachel's mood, and full of historical interest. Jeremy had joined her and Marjorie for their trip to the Acropolis, which was as spectacular as they had expected it to be. Octavia had remained on board ship, complaining of a headache. Rachel feared the loss of Wilfred had started to sink in and, although she didn't want to speculate, she didn't think the marriage would survive what had happened.

Jeremy appeared relaxed; the happiest she had ever seen him, probably helped by Marjorie's agreeing to Harvey Fanston's proposed investment. At least his money worries would be gone, if not his marital ones. The exports Lord Fanston wanted to add to the business were all legal and above board, according to Marjorie, who had succumbed to a business meeting early that morning. Lord Fanston, she said, had been extremely grateful to them for unearthing the killer and for his newfound liberty, although he was saddened by his sister-in-law's merciless killing spree. Tom had sent them both bouquets of flowers, which were waiting in their rooms following their outing, along with a simple message of thanks. There was another marriage Rachel had no doubt would soon come to an end, with or without Grandma Elrod's approval.

Rachel mulled over the events since she'd boarded the ship ten days before. Two murders, jewellery theft and an attempted murder; all in a week's work? The one good thing that had come out of it was that Jeremy and Marjorie seemed much closer. She was happy for her friend, although a part of her wondered if Jeremy's business deal success had played a bigger part in that closeness than it should. Still, she was thankful.

She dressed for dinner, donning the new white dress Carlos had bought especially for her to wear in Athens.

"You will look every bit the Greek goddess, my darling," he had said when he gave it to her. "I'm just sorry I won't see you in it."

She looked in the mirror. He was right: she looked and felt great, apart from the ache in her heart from missing him. Blinking a tear from her eye, she grabbed her evening bag and made her way swiftly across the rear corridor to Marjorie's room.

Marjorie looked elegant and beautiful in a beige dress, her bright eyes dancing with excitement and anticipation. "You'll never guess what a surprise I have in store for you!"

Oh no, thought Rachel. *What now? I just want a quiet dinner.* "You'd better tell me. I don't think I can take too much more excitement."

"Captain Jenson's invited us for dinner. Tatum Rodman, the assistant cruise director, delivered the invitation personally. Apparently, he doesn't want our memories of dining with him to be a 'Captain's Dinner Cruise Murder!' Frankly, neither do I. The only downside is His Lordship will be there, and my wretched daughter-in-law, but thankfully, none of the Fanston party."

Rachel grinned. "That's the sort of surprise I can live with." She put out her arm for Marjorie to take. "Come on, then. Let's not keep the captain waiting."

This time, dinner was in the officers' dining room with a table set for eight. Rachel could see Dr Bentley was there as well as Waverley, but she couldn't work out who the eighth place was for.

"Isn't this wonderful?" said Marjorie as Jeremy appeared, taking her arm, and escorting her and Octavia to the table. Rachel was about to follow when someone appeared behind her.

"May I escort you to dinner?"

Rachel spun around, eyes filling up. "Carlos!"

He pulled her into his arms and kissed her unashamedly. When they separated, he pinned a red rose to her white dress.

"My beautiful goddess."

"But… how…?" Rachel could hardly speak. Marjorie's twinkle and Carlos's flashing eyes told her they had planned this surprise for some time.

"Lady Marjorie thought it a good idea if I joined you for the last leg of the tour." He held out his arm for her to take.

Captain Jenson stood. "Mr and Mrs Jacobi-Prince, welcome to my table. I trust dinner tonight will be memorable for all the right reasons."

"Hear, hear," said Marjorie.

"And I thought you said you weren't good at speeches, Captain," Rachel replied, heart bursting with happiness.

THE END

Author's Note

Thank you for reading *Captain's Dinner Cruise Murder*, the tenth book in my Rachel Prince Mystery series. If you have enjoyed it, please leave an honest review on Amazon and/or any other platform you may use. I love receiving feedback from readers.

Keep in touch:

Signup for my no-spam newsletter and receive a FREE novella. You will also receive news of new releases and special offers, and have the opportunity to enter competitions.

Join now:

   https://www.dawnbrookespublishing.com

Follow me on Facebook:

   https://www.facebook.com/dawnbrookespublishing/

Follow me on Twitter:

   @dawnbrookes1

Follow me on Pinterest:

https://www.pinterest.co.uk/dawnbrookespublishing

Books by Dawn Brookes

Rachel Prince Mysteries

A Cruise to Murder

Deadly Cruise

Killer Cruise

Dying to Cruise

A Christmas Cruise Murder

Murderous Cruise Habit

Honeymoon Cruise Murder

A Murder Mystery Cruise

Hazardous Cruise

Captain's Dinner Cruise Murder

Corporate Cruise Murder (Coming soon 2022)

Carlos Jacobi PI

Body in the Woods

The Bradgate Park Murders

Murder at the Jewry Wall (Coming soon 2022)

Lady Marjorie Snellthorpe Mysteries

Death of a Blogger (Prequel Novella)

Murder at the Opera House

Murder in the Highlands (Coming soon 2022)

Memoirs

Hurry up Nurse: memoirs of nurse training in the 1970s
Hurry up Nurse 2: London calling
Hurry up Nurse 3: More adventures in the life of a student nurse

Picture Books for Children

Ava & Oliver's Bonfire Night Adventure
Ava & Oliver's Christmas Nativity Adventure
Danny the Caterpillar
Gerry the One-Eared Cat
Suki Seal and the Plastic Ring

Acknowledgements

Thank you to my editor Alison Jack, as always, for her kind comments about the book and for suggestions, corrections and amendments that make it a more polished read.

Thanks to my beta readers for comments and suggestions, and for their time given to reading the early drafts and to my ARC team – I couldn't do without you.

Thanks to my immediate circle of family and friends, who are so patient with me when I'm absorbed in my fictional world, for your continued support in all my endeavours.

I have to say thank you to my cruise-loving friends for joining me on some of the most precious experiences of my life, and to all the cruise lines for making every holiday a special one.

About the Author

Award winning author, Dawn Brookes holds an MA in Creative Writing with Distinction and is author of the Rachel Prince Mystery series, combining a unique blend of murder, cruising, and medicine with a touch of romance. A spinoff series with Lady Marjorie Snellthorpe taking the lead is in progress with the prequel novella, *Death of a Blogger* available in eBook, paperback and as an audiobook.

She also writes crime fiction featuring a tenacious PI which may be of interest to fans of Rachel Jacobi-Prince.

Dawn has a 39-year nursing pedigree and takes regular cruise holidays, which she says are for research purposes! She brings these passions together with a Christian background and a love of clean crime to her writing.

The surname of Rachel Prince is in honour of her childhood dog, Prince, who used to put his head on her knee while she lost herself in books.

Dawn's bestselling memoirs outlining her nurse training are available to buy. *Hurry up Nurse: memoirs of nurse training in the 1970s, Hurry up Nurse 2: London calling,* and *Hurry up*

Nurse 3: More adventures in the life of a student nurse. Dawn worked as a hospital nurse, midwife, district nurse and community matron across her career. Before turning her hand to writing for a living, she had multiple articles published in professional journals and coedited a nursing textbook.

She grew up in Leicester, later moved to London and Berkshire, but now lives in Derby. Dawn holds a Bachelor's degree with Honours and a Master's degree in education. Writing across genres, she also writes for children. Dawn has a passion for nature and loves animals, especially dogs. Animals will continue to feature in her children's books, as she believes caring for animals and nature helps children to become kinder human beings.

Printed in Great Britain
by Amazon